Horror Between the Sheets
Copyright © Cthulhu Sex, 2005

Stories copyright by the individual authors

All rights reserved

Published by Two Backed Books,
an imprint of Raw Dog Screaming Press
Landover Hills, MD

First Paperback Edition

Cover image: "Rift" by Michael Amorel, www.michaelamorel.com
Book design: Michael Amorel

Printed in the United States of America

ISBN 1-933293-01-2

Library of Congress Control Number 2005900688

Without limiting the rights under copyright reserved above, no part of this publication may be reproduced, stored in or introduced into a retrieval system, or transmitted, in any form, or by any means (electronic, mechanical, photocopying, recording, or otherwise), without the prior written permission of both the copyright owner and the above publisher of this book.

PUBLISHER'S NOTE:
This is a work of fiction. Names, characters, places and incidents either are the product of the author's imagination or are used fictitiously, and any resemblance to actual persons, living or dead, business establishments, events, or locales is entirely coincidental.

If you purchased this book without a cover, you should be aware that this book is stolen property. It was reported as "unsold and destroyed" to the publisher and neither the author nor the publisher has receeived any payment for this "stripped book."

www.twobackedbooks.com
www.cthulhusex.com

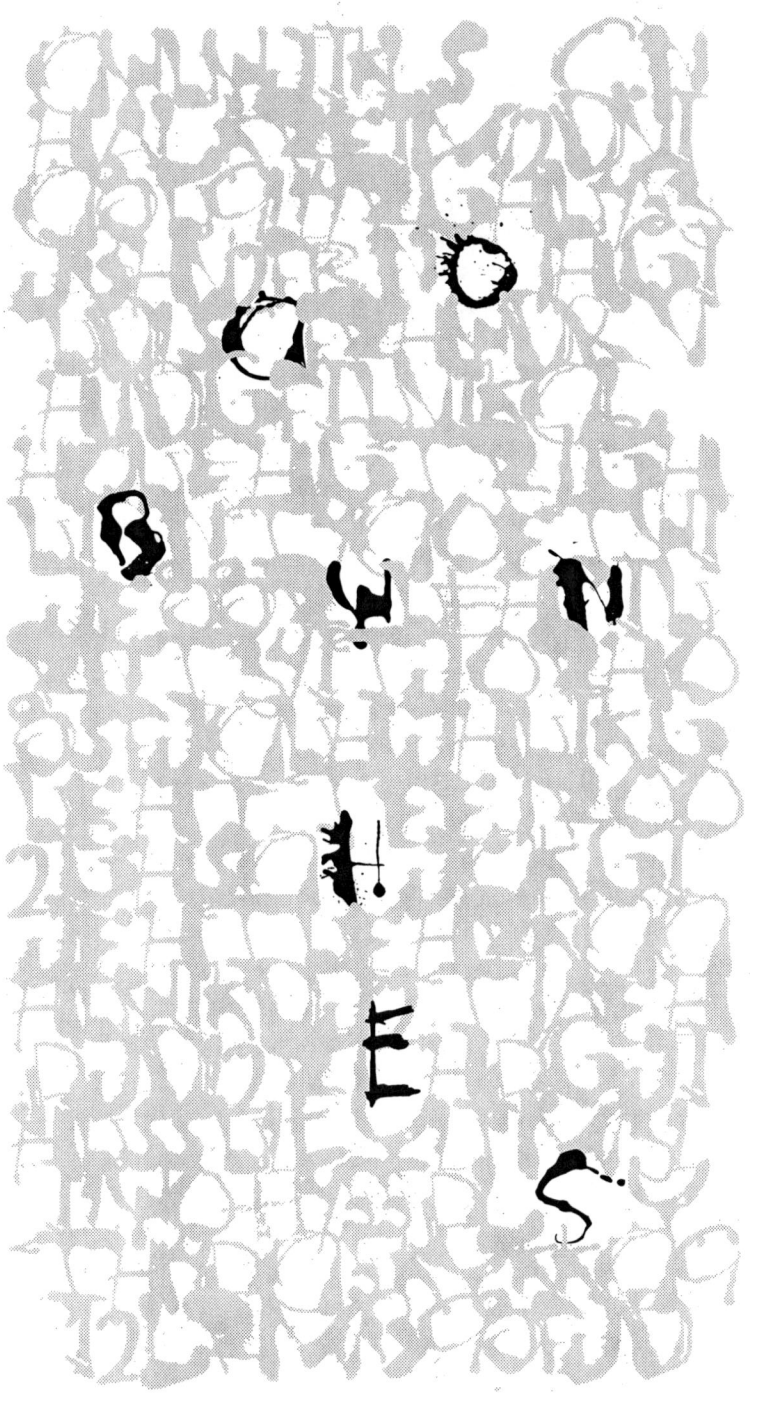

Horror Between the Sheets
Copyright © Cthulhu Sex, 2005

Stories copyright by the individual authors:
19 © Father Baer, 2000
Beyond © Brian Knight & Durant Haire, 2003
Cthulhu Sex (ahem!) —a poem— © Katherine Morel, 1998
de sade begs to differ © MorrisoN, 2003
Elegy in a Graveyard © Lynne den Hartog, 2001
Erato's Sister © David Annandale, 2003
Giant Squid! © Heather Highfield, 2000
Go Team © Kenneth Brady, 2003
He © Abigail Parsley, 1998
Masterpiece, The © Jenn Mann, 1998
Noseeums, The © Jeremy Russell, 2002
Pear, The © Matthew Howe, 1999
Phone Company, The © Racheline Maltese, 1998
Possession © Julie Shiel, 2002
Reaching Wall, The © Christine Morgan, 2003
Romancing the Worm © Sue D'Nimm, 2002
Siren © David Galef, 2003
Skin © Joi A. Brozek, 1996
Slice of Life, A © Arthur Cullipher, 2002
Titterer in the Twilight, The © Mark McLaughlin, 2003
Thaw © David Ethan Levit, 2001
Two Loves © Adam Falik & Robert Wheeler, 2000
Wandering in the Graveyard at Night © William Mordore, 2003

All rights reserved

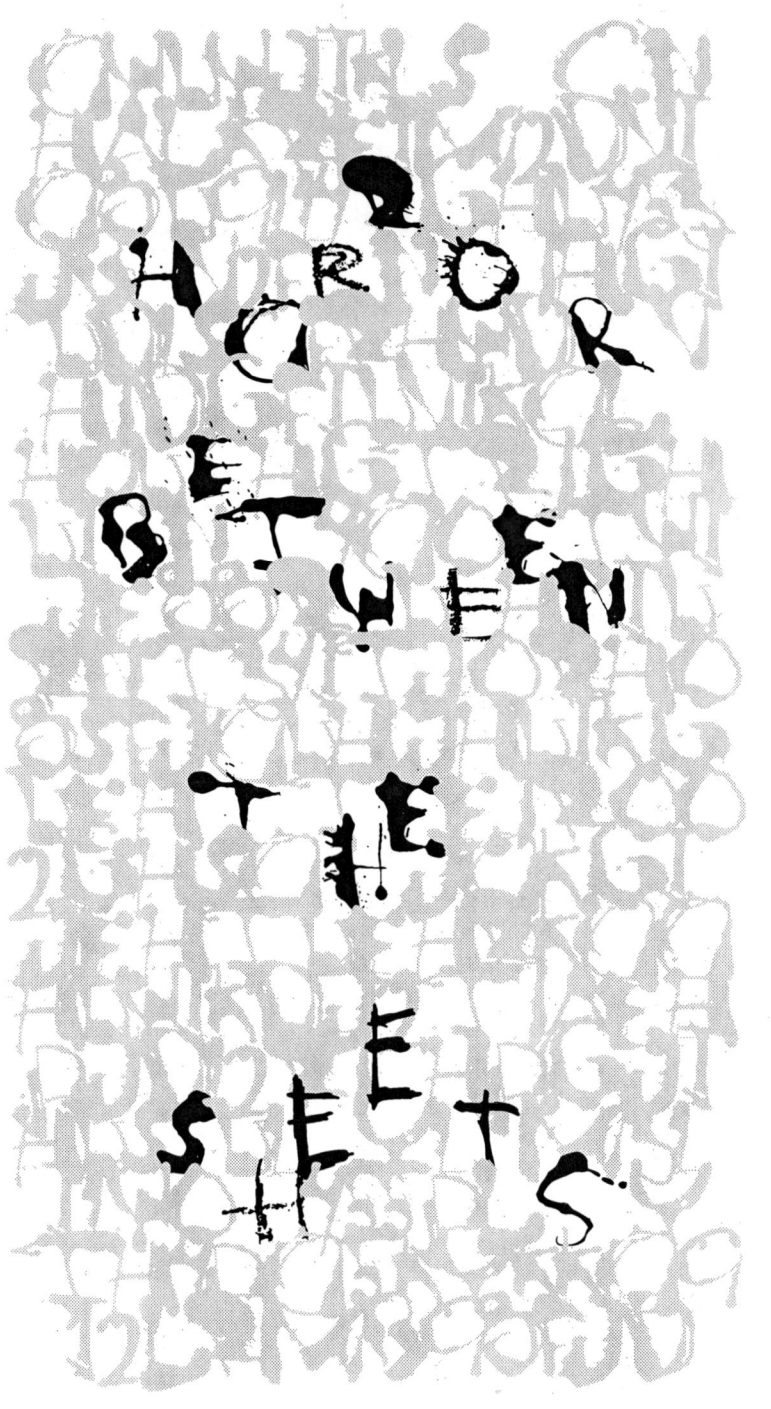

CONT

Introduction
by Michael Amorel iv

The Noseeums
by Jeremy Russell 3

The Titterer in the Twilight
by Mark McLaughlin 13

Erato's Sister
by David Annandale 15

Siren
by David Galef 23

Go Team
by Kenneth Brady 25

Cthulhu Sex (ahem!) —a poem—
by Katherine Morel 37

Beyond
by Brian Knight & Durant Haire 39

Elegy in a Graveyard
by Lynne den Hartog 59

A Slice of Life
by Arthur Cullipher 61

de sade begs to differ
by MorrisoN 71

Romancing the Worm
by Sue D'Nimm 75

ENTS

Thaw
  by David Ethan Levit 83

Skin
  by Joi A. Brozek 85

19
  by Father Baer 97

The Reaching Wall
  by Christine Morgan 99

Possession
  by Julie Shiel 113

The Masterpiece
  by Jenn Mann 115

Wandering in the Graveyard at Night
  by William Mordore 121

The Phone Company
  by Racheline Maltese 125

He
  by Abigail Parsley 133

Giant Squid!
  by Heather Highfield 143

Two Loves
  by Adam Falik & Robert Wheeler 145

The Pear
  by Matthew Howe 155

INTRODUCTION
BY MICHAEL AMOREL

Greetings and welcome to *Horror Between the Sheets*, the first collected works from *Cthulhu Sex Magazine*.

Thank you, reader, for purchasing *Horror Between the Sheets*. A special thanks goes to all the writers for creating these fantastic pieces and being involved with this project. I would like to thank everyone involved in the creative process of putting this project together, particularly Oliver Baer, Benjamin X. Wretlind, John Edward Lawson, Jennifer Barnes, Luke Crane and the love of my life, Jenn Mann. And last, but not least, I would like to thank all the writers, artists and readers who have supported *Cthulhu Sex Magazine* over the years. *Horror Between the Sheets* is dedicated to all those who have passed through the veil during the process of creating *Cthulhu Sex Magazine*, specifically the Davidsons, Per Christian Malloch and generally Oliver's receptionists, various members of our sales staff and our seasonal sacrifices.

Introduction — Michael Amorel

If you are like most normal people, I recommend you skip over the rest of this introduction and get straight to the good stuff, starting with page 2. You probably wouldn't want to stick around for an introduction anyway. It just tells about the making of this book, the historical significance of guanometers and some editor's self-important thoughts. After you read everything else, put the book in the bathroom so you can read the intro if you forget to bring whatever you really wanted to read. For now, just go on and skip ahead.

If you happen to be a contributor to the magazine and are upset that your piece didn't get picked, we recommend that you save time by skipping the intro, pretending that you did read it and angrily tossing the book at a wall a good enough distance away that it impacts with a satisfyingly solid thud. If your goad is still up, possible salvation can be found in:

—Dedicating your life and worldly goods to the Avatar of *Cthulhu Sex*.

—Writing a really, really excellent story and submitting it to *Cthulhu Sex Magazine*. (Because that would stick it to us, wouldn't it?)

—Plotting revenge and then committing suicide because the whole idea of getting even is fruitless, since we are too powerful for you.

—And lastly, you could actually read on and find out if you're at least named in the introduction. (If you aren't, then you should try one of the aforementioned ire-reductions.)

The works you are about to enjoy were taken from the pages of the complete *Cthulhu Sex Magazine* Volume I as well as Issues 13-15 of Volume II, also known as the black and white issues due to their black and white covers. In those 16 issues, we presented over 250 pieces of artwork, poetry, prose, comic and other indefinable works. Distilling their essences down to quantify their ability to hold up a "Best of" status was a long and arduous process.

Like any good organization, the first thing to do was to decide who would decide the final decision. After a weeklong rumble that ranged from the streets of Brooklyn to bayous of New Orleans and back again, three survivors emerged victorious, their gore-spackled bodies glinting ruddily in the setting sun as they stood on the corpses of their foes. They were Benjamin X. Wretlind, the Decimator of Incontinence, Oliver Baer, the Master of the Dangling Participle, and I, Michael Amorel, Maker-upper of Words.

Victorious, we ritually slathered the silken *Souzier* in clarified rancid llama butter obtained from the holy monks of *Xucthaluxha*, whose citadel of suffering sits high on top a jagged peak in the Andes. The *Souzier* then digested page after page of writings from a horribly mangled stack of well-molded back issues. Seams were slit, papers were shredded and sheaves of flattened flesh were feasted upon. Good times were had by all.

Next came the stringy discombobulation of important written matter from effluvium. Luckily, the effluvious matter was miasmal and softly fluttered away in its own stale vapor. But the piles of regurgitated paste were thick with mucus and needed dedicated hands to sift the diamonds from the pulp. Having no other recourse, we took the night off and invited a number of important people over for an orgy involving chocolate and marshmallows while we allowed the Vomina to do what they do best with the piles. Despite the high political and religious offices of Vomina members, or maybe because of it, they have uncompromising expertise when it comes to offal, emeses and regurgitation.

On the morning of the second day, we were greeted with a distilled pile of gems from the issues as well as two more bodies to add to the dedication. The delightful pieces chosen for possible publication were still many more than we could find flesh to print on. Mr. Wretlind was involved in the disposal of the new bodies and couldn't help us cull the remaining herd. Therefore, Mr. Baer and I enlisted the help of the *Cthulhu Sex Magazine* Motivatrix, Jenn Mann, to single out the most pristine pieces. At this point, each work cut was mourned by a thousand eyeless children, their wails lifting our sadness into the cold night winds to be carried throughout the

Introduction — Michael Amorel

dreams of innocents. The excellent pieces that didn't survive this process of vivisection are too numerous to describe in detail here, but they included the glorious "Gutter Lover" by John Edward Lawson, the disturbing "Kids" by Wrath James White, the unusual "Elbow" by Hertzan Chimera & Alex Severin, the entertaining "Come and Gone" by Amy Grech and the first piece that was submitted to us via internet, "Why I Want to Fuck Cthulhu" by Dan Clore.

What we were left with was the cream of the crop, precious gems so wondrous that they would be set in The Crown of the Avatar and displayed for all to see. To prepare for that, we polished them, making sure that every speck of *Souzier* lubrication was carefully put aside for later use. Then we made the authors jump through flaming hoops of legalese for our master's enjoyment. Tossing the sparse comfort of cold hard coin at their whipped, bleeding and exposed backsides, we lasciviously thanked them for their services. Finally, their words were branded onto these thinly beaten sheets of fine human flesh, which were perfect bound and shipped into your hands. The good people at Two Backed Books were quite helpful in treating the pages with the proper coatings.*

Now that you know the back story of this collection, let me give you some pointers on what you may or may not know about the authors and poets within.

> A) We have collected a short paragraph before each piece, generally written by the author, with information they would like you to know about them. Some of them have been open enough to give you a web address so you can learn even more. I suggest that you visit them. In this day and age of instant gratification via the internet, it would be foolish to waste valuable space here with duplicating such important information.
>
> 2) There are writers in this anthology who are not necessarily who or what you think they are. Don't

*Readers with guanometers will know which pages are contaminated and should therefore be avoided.

take it for granted that the name or the information described in the introduction paragraph will give you hints as to which ones are straight forward normal humans and which ones are other things.

III) Scattered throughout this book are clues for those of you who have the Introcostial Decoder Ring, as given to you by the 2-3-2 Mistathrope. The first three people to come back to me with the right answer will receive their next level of blood badge for free as well as one practice stabbing.

We here at *Cthulhu Sex Magazine* appreciate your patronage and implore you to remember the last thing ever said by the last sacrifice before the one you're thinking of:

"The height of true sensual experience is only a gory, putrescent, fetid fleshwad away from the heart."

Tentacles,

Michael Amorel
Avatar of *Cthulhu Sex Magazine*

PS: Those of you who have no idea what any of this is about, but have not read the collected works herewithin, do not worry. The rest of this is quite good, really. If you have read the collected works herewithin and still have no idea what any of this is about, put down the book and slowly walk away. There is nothing to see here.

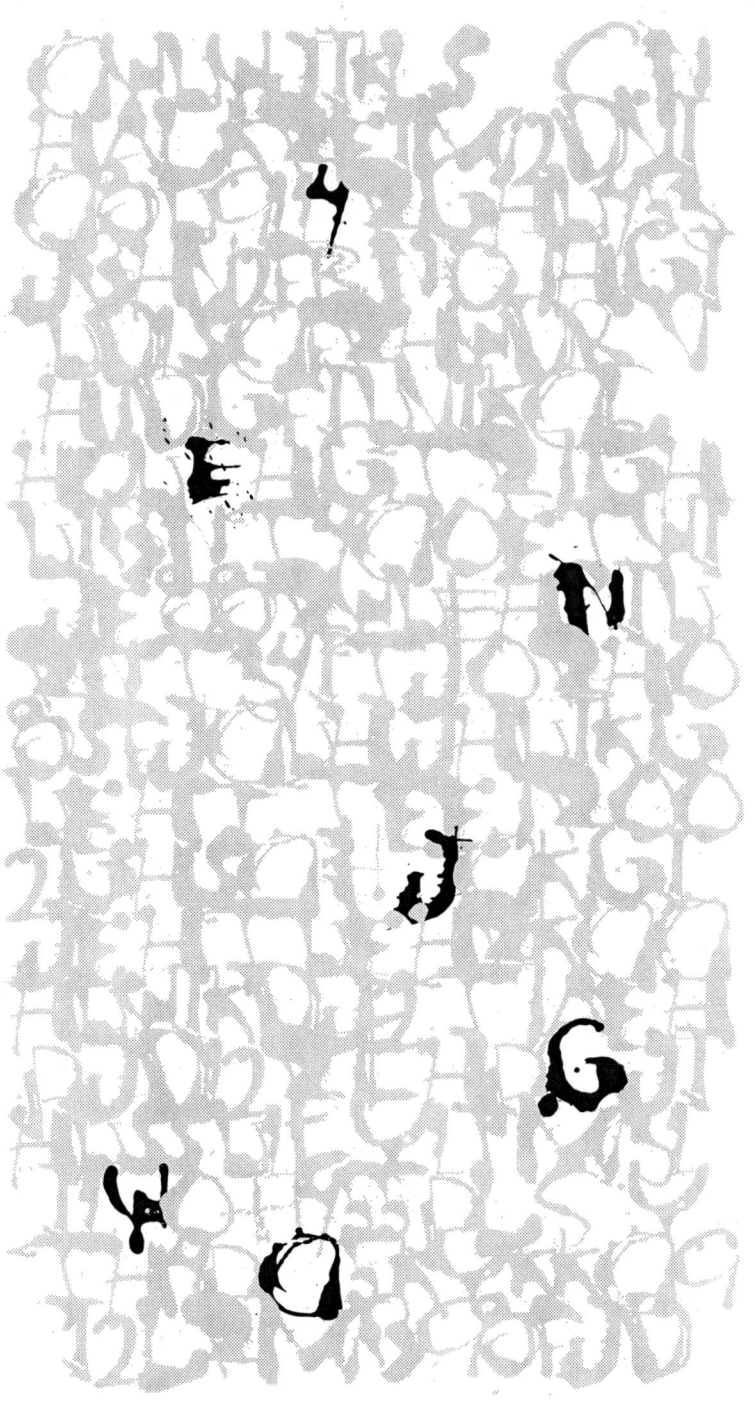

Jeremy Russell

Jeremy Russell is an award-winning freelance writer. His work has been published in the *San Francisco Bay Guardian*, *New York Press* and *American Book Review*, as well as a variety of trade press and indy 'zines. His fiction has been anthologized by Suspect Thoughts Press, Cyber Age Adventures and in *The Mammoth Book of Legal Thrillers* (Carroll & Graf). www.jeremyrussell.com

"The Noseeums" was originally printed in issue 24, volume I

The Noseeums
by Jeremy Russell

The bleak hospital corridor was empty. Heather stared down it all the way to the small glass window at the far end; daylight came through muted by translucent ripples and fractured by chicken wire. She moved her long brown hair out of her face, revealing pink, dimpled cheeks. She was a healthy-looking, plump woman in her forties wearing a simple pair of jeans, flannel shirt and an excess of strange necklaces, some beaded, others simply straps with amulets. Her eyes were open very wide. One of her hands crawled up her shirt to her neck and she began to rub her jugular vein slowly. She cocked her head a fraction of an inch, listening to the silence. In their sockets, her eyes moved to the left, bringing the pupils to rest half-buried. Then, she moved her head to the left as well. Gradually, her entire upper body turned around until she was looking backwards over her shoulder at nearly 180 degrees. Meanwhile, her hand continued to stroke the throbbing tissue in her neck underneath which the blood flowed back and forth between her heart and her brain.

Her mouth fell open and then the door burst at the far end of the hall.

The hallway was flooded with sound. Three orderlies, struggling with a male patient in tattered white garb, toppled into the room. Beneath their knees and fingers, the patient was squealing darkly about an abortion. Presently a doctor, her red hair held back in a scrunchie, stepped out with a hypodermic needle in her hand. The doctor sunk her needle into the tattered garments at the man's hip and he yelled a long guttural monosyllable that at last subsided into blubbering.

A nurse ran up beside Heather and took her arm. "I'm sorry about this, Mrs. Sparkman. Your husband is just this way." She turned Heather around and pulled her along.

After a moment, Heather said, "I can hear them."

"Hear who?"

"The patients."

"Oh no you can't. Walls are soundproof." She nodded as if she were imparting a facility secret. "Nobody can hear the patients."

Heather was ushered into a waiting room divided in half by a glass wall like a window to the other side. "He'll be brought in to you. You can talk for a little while. But he has to go back in twenty minutes."

"I know."

The nurse left her alone then. She sat quietly, moving her hands back and forth in her lap. At first, she gazed up at another of those translucent chicken-wire windows. Then, her head sagged and she stared down the long distance over the folds of her jeans to the blue and brown tops of her Hi-Tech sneakers. Unconsciously, she began to hum. Clear liquid built up on her eyelashes.

When the door on the other side of the glass wall opened, she jerked, straightening her back, and wiped her eyes. Two orderlies led her husband in.

He had a great deal of facial hair this time. With it, his short round body looked ridiculous in the white garments. But there was still a twinkle in his eyes. The orderlies nudged him into a seat across from her. Beneath all that beard, he smiled. His fingers could be seen at the edges of the sleeves, rubbing cloth frantically between forefinger and thumb.

She looked at him for a long time. "Well?"

"Not yet," he said, his voice projected at her from a speaker. "I just want to look at you for awhile."

They both stared at each other through the glass. At last, she said, "I can hear the other patients, but not you."

His smile broadened. "I've finally perfected unhearability."

"Is that even possible?"

"With Thorazine, it becomes almost easy."

She reached out with the listening part of her mind, but it was like being in a room with a cadaver. There wasn't even the white noise of a coma patient. Finally, with a forced clearing of her throat, she adjusted her shirt and set aside her amazement. "I've come about the house," she said. "The Institute finally collected all of your papers and I've completed negotiations with the Preternatural Studies Department for them to care for the recordings and video material. They want to put together some kind of cable access documentary. Don't worry, part of the agreement was that they were not to mention us specifically. Our findings will be called the results of studies by independent researchers." She paused. "Oh yes, and that anthropology professor at Rutgers accepted the donation of relics and artifacts. They'll pick everything up next week and the house will be empty. I sold most of the library off ages ago now. I... Kevin, I can't keep the house."

No longer smiling, he nodded. "I understand."

"Do you understand that this is your last chance? Our last shot at picking up where we left off. Once we give up the house, that's it, it's over. I'm not going to continue to wait for you." She closed her eyes and tilted her head so that her chin touched her chest. The tears brimmed again. "Why do you stay?"

He pushed his hand towards the door. "Too many windows out there, too easy to creepy-crawl. Here there are so many locked doors and backup systems for the lights."

"We can find a place like this, deep in an apartment building. We could have a generator. Safety can be bought."

He looked down. "Here it's best... They can't ever get me."

She leaned forward in her chair, looking him in the eye. "I don't believe in them."

"That doesn't change the fact that they're real."

She looked at him like she didn't believe him. The twinkle flashed in his eyes. She tapped one finger against her knee. "Okay."

"What?"

"Okay, I want to see them. Now, right now." She slapped both her knees with sudden violence. "I want to see them right now, Kevin, god dammit." The necklaces jumped.

For a long time, he didn't respond. He seemed fascinated by the backs of his hands and the knuckles in particular, which he kept in constant sluggish motion as if squeezing an invisible ball. When he raised his head, his brow and eyes had collapsed together in a collision of anguish and guilt. "You know I'm sane?" This was both a statement and a question.

"I don't know anything. You're in here, after all."

"Yes, but I'm not crazy."

"Then, you can leave. You have no reason to stay. And the cost..." She stopped herself. They both knew it wasn't about the money. She covered her face with her hand, rubbing her temples with her middle finger and thumb. "They are not real."

"The noseeums —"

"Dammit, Kevin, noseeums are sand flies. Just flies. Not... invisible creatures."

He smiled wanly. "I know that. What these are, they're like starfish, but they have six legs and, I know how ridiculous this sounds, but each leg grows to a tapering end, which sprouts other tapering ends, which sprout still others, like tree branches, and in the middle, where they're thick like a heart muscle, they have a mouth and above it, one small dark eye. Altogether, they have a vaguely spiraled shape, almost a fractal, and their blue-black skin, like the hide of a seal, pulses."

Heather took a deep breath. She scratched furiously behind her ear. "Okay, let's say that I believe you. That these... noseeums... are real. Then why can't I hear them? I hear everything else, except you now. They aren't nohearums too, are they? Don't they make sounds?"

"Sounds, yes," he said. "They think-move. It's kind of like the crisp whisper of a bug under dry leaves or the soft scuttle of a crab across the sand. But, you probably don't hear it for the same reason that you stop hearing the hum of a computer when you've been around it awhile, because... out there," he motioned his head at the wall, "they are everywhere."

"Fine. Okay. Let's say I accept all this. Although you haven't a shred of proof." She paused and then brightened. "But you could show me, couldn't you? The same way that you taught me to listen?"

"No. I could, perhaps, but I won't."

"Why not?"

He tugged at his beard fretfully. "Once you can see them... they can see you."

She rolled her eyes and snorted. "Isn't that convenient. You can't prove it to me, because you want to protect me."

He shrugged.

"You know what I think," she said. "I think you're just paranoid."

Without changing his expression, he licked at some dry skin in the corner of his mouth. Then he said, "Just because you're paranoid, doesn't mean that they're not after you." Then he held up his hand as if to ward off a punch. "I might be able to help you hear them, but I'd rather not, because of what they are."

"Which is?"

"Hunger. The hunger at the center of life. Pure hunger. Almost the Platonic form of hunger. They're always fighting and killing one another in flocks like vicious, malevolent pigeons. But they kill slowly, as if it was the killing and not the devouring that brought them the greatest pleasure. They kill to cause distress and they hunger not for each other's matter — indeed, what could such immaterial creatures offer in the way of nutrition? — but for pain, terror, the horrible dying bleats and, more than anything, the desperate thrashing. It's horrible to witness. Worse, it makes you realize the true nature... of fundamental consciousness... of reality. Do you remember Mr. Meadows?"

"Carl Meadows? How could I forget after the way you obsessed over him? You even hired that private detective."

"It was because I saw him die."

"So you said at the time. Of course, people die every day, so I never understood the significance of it. You didn't even know him."

"When I saw Carl die, I was seeing them, too. It was very early on and they were still ignoring me and I was still only curious." He pinched the end of his nose, then wiped his fingers on his shirt. "I was walking through the park, just taking it all in. And the noseeums were everywhere, mounded up as high as my knees in some places, fighting, biting, like a panorama from Dante's Inferno. It was a hot day, too. June third, I think. A lot of people had come down to the park with their kids. A lot of dogs. Carl was sitting on a bench with a vacant smile on his face and I remember paying special attention to him because the noseeums crowded around his bench appeared to be watching him, waiting for something.

"When the heart attack hit, I was looking somewhere else, but I was close enough to hear him gasp. I mean to hear his..."

"I know what you mean."

"When I looked, he was on his back under the bench. He must have fallen off and rolled backwards. I saw him separate from himself. I saw his... spirit. It was free for a second. Naked. Quite a bit younger appearing than he had been, like a snapshot of him in his prime. His spirit had a moment to look about, to realize, and then they swarmed over it. And in an instant they had him, as though in death he had somehow become tangible to them. They... they pulled him down and..." Tears leapt into Kevin's eyes. "They had him for about, oh, I don't know." His voice was thick. "It seemed like forever." He sighed, bowed, seemed to draw himself back in. Tears were rolling down his sideburns into his beard. "I became obsessed because I wanted to believe that, that it was... I wanted to believe it was his fault. Maybe if he'd been a bad man, maybe I could have convinced myself that he'd deserved that end and that it wasn't what I really thought it was. But in all my searching, I couldn't find anyone who would say that. No one said he was perfect, but he certainly wasn't evil. He was just a person like you or me and... do you see?"

"See what?"

"What that means. His fate, his end, that's what awaits us all. That's — forget the tunnel of light — this is what really happens. We are devoured by noseeums, nothing more than a cause for a feeding frenzy before the final disintegration of our beings. The cleanup crew for the afterlife. Soul maggots."

"But why do you think you'll be safe in here?"

He tapped his leg meaningfully. "You ever notice how ghosts are never outside, how they always haunt buildings?" His hand shot up as if he was just realizing what he was about to say himself. "That is why ghosts are always slamming doors."

"That's... that's... you're hiding here to escape supernatural... piranha?" She was laughing, but mirthlessly. "Anything else you want to tell me?" She abruptly uncrossed her legs as if to stand. "Schizophrenic, I'll say when people ask. Saw things. And that'll be how I think of you from now until you die. I suppose I'll know for sure one way or the other someday, but by then it'll be too late. Too late for me. Too late for you."

He cocked his head, gritted his teeth and fixed her in a mad red glare, anger glowing out all over him.

And suddenly, she found herself hearing his mind clearly and it was so dark and noisome, so unlike the man she had known, that she nearly screamed.

Her instinct was to run, abandon the whole asylum, but she held on through a tide of nausea, listening with her mind. First, she listened to him and the black fear in him underwent synathesia from a whistling to the honeyed smell of rot. Then, as she had learned to do, she moved her mind through him. It was difficult to get past the putrescence inside his head, but eventually she thought there might be something else, unless that was only another facet of his illness. She jammed her eyes shut and gripped her hands together almost in prayer. What she heard was like monsters hissing at the window.

Then, it was the voice of the nurse, "Mrs. Sparkman?"

On the other side of the glass, a wide, blond man was leading Kevin out.

"The meeting's over, Mrs. Sparkman."

"I... okay." She stood up feeling woozy. Had it been real what she'd heard? And what had she heard anyway? She brushed herself off as if she'd been sitting in dirt.

The nurse led her into the hall and, pulling at her ear thoughtfully, Heather looked each way down blank corridors. Feeling deaf, she began to pull her ear harder. The nurse was now several steps ahead of her.

Then Heather heard some sobbing, soft and far away. It seemed to echo at her and break like a quiet wave. There was something about it that frightened her and she hurried after the nurse, her necklaces swaying over her flannel shirt. Dropping her hand from her ear to hold the many amulets still, she moved past a door. The sound beyond it, which she heard with her mind, was like someone screaming into a pillow. It made her stop, but disappeared as soon as she looked directly at the door. When she turned away, it started again at a distinct increase. She fell back and looked again. This time the screaming did not fade away, but seemed to rise up out of the pillow and throw itself right against the door.

The nurse had disappeared. Heather's heart leapt against her ribs like a jackrabbit in a cage. She ran.

The hallways rolled by empty, awful and fused with the various sounds from each of the various rooms: the rumble of a man's lonely masturbation; the call of a feral girl with her teeth on her fingers, biting at the ends of her nails; the sigh of a pederast sticking himself with a stolen needle; the crying of a rapist whose mother had died yesterday of cancer; the blank snap of a thoughtless invalid. Each door was alive with the tumult of its occupant's psyche, each sound a statement about the sufferer's affliction.

At last, Heather came to a stop at the far end of a hall, all the voices and noises crawling like spiders on the back of her skull. Sweat poured over her dimples. She cursed her telepathic ability, not for the first time, although this was uniquely intense as if Kevin had opened her further than ever. Covering her eyes with her hands, she prepared to be overcome by the sounds.

Then they were gone.

When she opened her eyes, the nurse was standing before her, looking both concerned and angry. Heather opened her mouth to apologize, but couldn't speak. The nurse waited. Finally, Heather said, "Please, show me the way out." And all the way, the sound she'd heard in Kevin's mind followed her like a snake, or something else, slithering to keep up.

Mark McLaughlin

Mark McLaughlin is an unspeakable ancient entity from beyond the boundaries of time and space. Turn-ons: mindless rampaging, hellish orgies of destruction, and long, moonlit walks on the beach. Turn-offs: the powers of light, goodness and salvation... as well as people who reveal the endings of movies. Collections of his fiction include *Once Upon A Slime*, *Hell Is Where The Heart Is* and *Motivational Shrieker*. Also, he is the co-author (with Rain Graves and David Niall Wilson) of *The Gossamer Eye*, which won a Bram Stoker Award for Superior Achievement in Poetry. Visit Mark on the web at www.geocities.com/mcmonstrous.

"The Titterer In the Twilight" was originally printed in issue 14, volume II

The Titterer in the Twilight

by Mark McLaughlin

Really and for true
is it a merciful happenstance
that humanity is composed of
a motley melange of scoundrels,
ne'er-do-wells, jackanapes
and perfidious miscreants.
The lot of them are absorbed
in a riotous cornucopia of
superficial intrigues and diversions
and so, would be blissfully unaware
if, say, some writhing, giggling entity
from beyond the sane boundaries
of time, space and good taste —
some vile and malignant titterer
in the twilight — were suddenly
to descend upon civilization,
hoping to turn its inhabitants
into bipedal livestock, reducing
our cities to pathetic cattleyards
of fear, torment, lingering death
and eternal damnation. Of course,
all that is mere conjecture.
Speculation. Supposition. I'm sure
that really, there is no such critter
who so dearly loves to titter,
squirming in the shadows, waiting
to wrap its unspeakable tentacles
around your pale, trembling throat.
Still, just to be on the safe side,
don't order the calimari.

David Annandale

David Annandale has written horror fiction most of his life. His stories most recently have appeared in *Wild Things Live There: The Best of Northern Frights*, *The Asylum Volume 2: The Violent Ward* and *Dead But Dreaming*. His novels, *Crown Fire* and *Kornukopia*, are published by Turnstone Press.

"Erato's Sister" was originally printed in issue 13, volume II

Erato's Sister

by David Annandale

He didn't think he'd be into it. But she surprised him, Larry gave her that. He'd been right about one thing, though. She was different.

Larry had met Evelyn at The Keg. He'd cruised in after work, the week's aggravating assfucks sloughed off, a weekend's potential the wide horizon ahead. It was after seven and the lounge was packed. The air was a smog of hormone effluvia. There was no prey here, only predators. Cougars and wolves, dot-commers and civil servants, all of them preening, flexing, tarting, posturing, everyone and Aunt Penny's monkey out for the sweat, for the clash of flesh in flesh, for the discharge and the scream. Larry scanned the crowd, open to suggestion. The right shape of calf, flick of hair, or turn of lips might settle the weekend. He was ready for adventure.

He knew he'd found adventure when he saw her, a litheness of dark hair and darker eyes. Even in the sea of armed loins, she stood out, enveloped by the perfect Zen of the supreme hunter. She was sitting at a booth, eating, and she was alone. The wolves seemed to be steering clear. Perhaps she'd slashed a few muzzles. Perhaps they were scared of a disruption of the food chain, a disruption that would hurt. Larry wasn't worried. The danger haze excited him. He went over to make himself prey.

She had two plates in front of her. One was ribs, the other chicken wings. She was a messy eater. Her fingers were covered in juice, grease and barbecue sauce. Her lips were smeared. Her napkin was still rolled up around the ignored cutlery. Normally, Larry would have been put off. But what was it that hooked and reeled him in, that had his cock twitching with interest? Was it the fact that she clearly didn't give a flying fuck? Was it the contrast of the meat smears on skin with the immaculate, grey, miniskirted power suit? He wasn't sure. He didn't care. He said, "Can I join you?"

She paused, a wing in her mouth. She eyed him up and down, sucking slowly on the wing. She put the wing down and held out a hand. "Evelyn," she said.

"Larry." He didn't hesitate. He shook her hand and felt his become slick with the grease. Their fingers slipped against each other.

Evelyn smiled. "Have a seat, Larry." She picked up a rib, licked it, then, mouth open, scraped the meat off with her teeth. Sauce dribbled down her chin. "Tell me," she said. "Hottest movie you know."

"*Tom Jones.*"

Her grin, tiger-like, grew. "Good answer. Playing to your audience, Larry? Pandering?"

"Just want to see where this is heading."

Her gaze, concertina wire. If he lied, he'd be sliced. "You're asking to be tested."

"Try me."

She chuckled once, deep in her throat. There was a dollop of barbecue sauce on her right index finger. She rubbed it lightly with her thumb, then moved her hand to her chest, razor eyes on Larry the whole time. She pinched a nipple, leaving a brown splotch on her white blouse, spotless until now. "Tell me what you are," she said.

"Hard." He was. Dirty, he was thinking. Fucking dirty. He wanted to see the clothes tear.

"Good. Stay that way." Still staring at him, she picked up a wing. She lifted one leg up, resting her foot on the bench beside her, knee bare, thigh bare as the skirt slipped. Larry now noticed that she wasn't wearing stockings. Her hand and the wing disappeared beneath the table. Larry couldn't see where she was putting the meat, but her skirt slipped down still further.

"Is that a good idea?" he asked. He didn't really believe she was doing this. He glanced around. He saw a woman two tables over staring their way, face blanching. He looked back at Evelyn. "That's dangerous."

"Not for me." She blinked once, slowly, with pleasure, then brought the wing back up and handed it to Larry. She cocked her head and waited.

She didn't, Larry thought, not really. He sniffed the wing. Christ Jesus, she had. She was still looking at him, testing. He smiled at her and ate the wing. As he did so, he felt her toe his crotch with her other foot. He was still hard.

"Good man," Evelyn said.

They went to her place. Larry lived closer, walking distance, but she insisted. She drove. He didn't recognize the make of her car. It was a sleek, black switchblade and just getting into it felt like maximum risk. She drove it with intent to harm, a dark wolf among sheep. In seconds, Larry was hyperventilating with fear and desire.

"How good is your fantasy life?" Evelyn asked. She overtook a Corolla, cutting back so fast the other car had to slam on its brakes. She glanced in the rear-view mirror and smirked.

"As good as the next guy's," Larry answered.

"That's all?"

"It gets me by."

"Thrilling."

"But you're inspiring me to new heights."

Evelyn laughed. She roared. She laughed so hard she almost went off the road. Her laugh sucked up all the air in the car and its echo filled all the space. Larry tried to grin, but Evelyn's mirth left no room for his. He was startled. He hadn't thought he'd been that funny.

Evelyn finally stopped laughing. Her smile, a hook in itself and twice as deadly, was back. "If I don't inspire you," she said, "I'm really falling down on the job."

She lived on 112th Street, on the fringes of the river valley that bisected the city. The area had been wealthy in the Twenties, had hit the skids in the Sixties and was re-gentrifying. Her house was the last on the street and overlooked the valley. The yard was overgrown and the house was a giant, decaying molar. Larry couldn't square it with the razored luxury of the car. He half-expected to go through the porch. Evelyn smiled at his expression. "I like character," she said and unlocked the door.

The inside was more comfortable. It wasn't fully restored, but Larry didn't think the floor was going to collapse. He smelled something cooking when they stepped in. "Somebody else here?" he asked. A threesome? Okay, but only if the third was another woman.

Evelyn shook her head. "Dinner. I left a pot roast on."

"You're a woman of healthy appetites."

"That's a matter of opinion." She walked away. "Why are you still dressed?" she asked without turning around.

Larry chuckled and followed her down the hall, shucking clothes as he went. Naked, he stood in the kitchen doorway, lightly stroking himself. Evelyn still didn't turn around. She opened the oven door, pulled out the roasting pan and placed it on the stove-top. Larry thought there was something odd about the way she did this, but before he could put his finger on the anomaly, she was tugging at her skirt with one hand. It tore as it came off and she tossed it away. She wasn't wearing panties. She stood with her legs spread, her stance a command. She still didn't look at Larry. She busied herself with the roast. "Eat me," she said.

Larry approached and got down on his knees. He kissed her ass, tonguing round flesh, and slowly worked his head between her thighs. His lips met hers. Her vagina was obscenely wet and it called his tongue. And there, mixed in with the taste of woman, was the unmistakable tang of barbecue sauce. My God, he thought, my God. She really did do it.

Her thighs clamped around his head as he licked, a clutch of casual strength. He heard her grunt with pleasure. He heard the clatter of cutlery. After a minute, she said, "Wait. Stop."

He sat back. She turned to face him. She'd been slicing the roast and her mouth was full of meat. She chewed and her mouth bled juice. She threw off the rest of her clothes and, still chewing, crouched over Larry. The smile became wide, so fierce Larry almost came. She ducked her head and swallowed his cock.

Larry's eyes bugged. Half-chewed roast and gravy swirled around his penis, tentacles of heat and liquid. Tongue searched, teeth nipped, Evelyn slurped and he couldn't help himself. He screamed, the sound an ecstasy of filth and pleasure. He slammed his palms against the floor, muscles going spastic in the disconnection of total abandonment. He felt the orgasm coming, Krakatoa.

Evelyn stopped. She sat up and swallowed. Larry gasped and reached for her. "You want more?" she asked.

"Oh Christ."

"Want to try something else?"

"Anything."

"Stand up."

He didn't think he could, but he managed it, clutching the kitchen counter for support. Evelyn took his cock in hand and led him towards the basement door. Her fingers moved as she walked, strobe-fast squeeze-release, and Larry almost screamed again. Evelyn threw open the door and took him downstairs. The rhythm of her fingers didn't stumble once.

Wracked by the pleasure, Larry took a few seconds to realize what he was seeing.

The basement was an unfinished space of grey concrete. It was full of beef carcasses hanging by chains and hooks. It was not refrigerated; it was heated. The smell of a greater ripeness plunged deep into Larry's lungs. Somehow, he just got harder. "What the fuuuuck?" he groaned.

"That's right," Evelyn whispered. "Fuck." She pulled Larry toward the nearest carcass. She stroked its flank with one hand, drove Larry to ecstasies of thunder with the other. "Expand your horizons." She licked the beef. She pulled her tongue away slowly and Larry saw clear liquid that was not her saliva link her to the meat. Then she kissed him and he tasted the corruption, and it was good. "Come on," she said, still whispering. She let go of him for a moment and cut a slit into the side of the beef with her fingernails. Cock throbbing, Larry watched the power of her fingers, looked at the china white of her hands and realized what had seemed wrong upstairs. She hadn't used oven mitts to handle the roasting pan. There was no sign of burn, no hint of charred flesh. Beat-beat, went Larry's heart.

Evelyn stepped behind him and pushed him towards the carcass. At the moment of embrace, he saw maggots in the meat. The whole slab was glistening with rot. He hugged it to him anyway, slamming his body up against warmth and wetness and softness and bone and weight. The chain squeaked and he and the beef moved together in a slaughterhouse two-step. Evelyn's chin was on his shoulder, her breath fetid porn in his ear. One of her hands slipped around his waist and slid his cock into the meat. "Fuck," she commanded, and he did, thrusting his cock deep into infinite flesh. He couldn't get close enough. Slime trickled down his legs. Beat-beat, went his heart, but he couldn't stop and the turn-on was seismic.

"Shall I tell you?" Evelyn purred, her breasts pressing into Larry's back, her cunt a slick presence against his ass.

"Yes," Larry gasped.

"You know there's a muse for erotic poetry. But that's such a narrow field. My prissy sister can have it. Now, where do you think the dark thoughts come from? The fantasies you shouldn't, shouldn't, shouldn't have, but you whack off to anyway." She nibbled his ear and her teeth felt sharp. "Who pushes you over the line? Who makes you fuck that line until it bleeds?"

"You," Larry said in worship.

"Feed me," she ordered and her teeth, fish hooks, sank into his shoulder all the way to the bone.

"Nnnngg," said Larry and he bit deep into the meat. Maggots squirmed around his teeth and tickled his palate. He vomited and shoved his face deeper into meat swimming in his own puke. He felt Evelyn tense with effort. There was a rippling and her embrace became impossible. Her arms stretched around both him and the beef. He could see her elbows three feet in front of him and there were still hands squeezing his thighs. He wanted to scream, but he hadn't come yet. He pumped the meat and Evelyn hugged them hard. There were new sounds now, not the sounds of flesh and juice, but cracks and snaps, the sounds of bone. Larry felt the beef's ribs sink into his sides. Heat spilled down his front and he pulled his head back from the beef to look down. His blood was everywhere.

"Fuck," Evelyn ordered, her voice gift, mantra and curse. There was a vibration in her throat, the pent-up pleasure of sex darker than the worst smile. She squeezed tighter yet and the carcass sliced Larry wide open. He was one with the meat. Two of Evelyn's hands snaked into his guts, fumbled and tugged. He grunted as he saw his large intestine yanked out. Evelyn slit the intestine, then pulled his cock out of the beef and slid it into his steaming condom. "Fuck," came the order again and, even though his body was snapping into chicken bone shrapnel, he did. And Evelyn surprised him, Larry gave her that.

He didn't think he'd be into it.

David Galef

David Galef has published poetry and fiction in magazines ranging from the old British *Punch* to the Czech *Prague Revue*, the Canadian *Prism International*, the American *Shenandoah*, *The Formalist*, *Light*, *The Laurel Review*, and many other places. He has also written the novels *Flesh* and *Turning Japanese*, the short-story collection *Laugh Track*, two children's books, two translations of Japanese proverbs, and literary criticism. His essays have appeared in *The New York Times*, *Newsday*, *The Village Voice*, *Twentieth Century Literature* and elsewhere. He's a professor of English at the University of Mississippi where he administers the M.F.A. program in creative writing.

"Siren" was originally printed in issue 14, volume II

SIREN

BY DAVID GALEF

She sells suffering by the ounce,
A substance quaintly labeled "sin,"
Her skirt hiked high to catch the breeze
And anything else that drifts on in.

She hawks little thorn-tipped kisses,
Attar of envy, pricks to pride,
On-your-knees humiliation,
Love darts sticking in your side,

Paralysis and sweet remorse,
Crippling blows to self-esteem,
Cigarette marks and burning desire,
A soft caress that's just a dream.

If pushed, she can perform real tricks.
One squeeze, a pinch of fairy dust,
Will shrink you down to plaything size
To seal you in a jar marked "lust."

Her list of clients knows no bounds:
All incomes, rank, and station.
Her range of pain is only matched
By your imagination.

Kenneth Brady

Kenneth Brady is a writer, actor, producer and director.

His short stories have appeared in magazines and anthologies around the world. Several of his stage plays have been produced, he's sold a screenplay and he's produced an independent feature film that has received several awards. He lives in Eugene, Oregon where he is a member of the Wordos. He has an almost unnatural fascination with rubber chickens. Find out more at www.sff.net/people/kennethbrady.

I drove by a school bus full of cheerleaders in Southern California and several of them flashed me. My first thought — well, OK, my second thought — was "What are they hiding that they would do that just to distract my attention?"

"Go Team" was originally printed in issue 14, volume II

Go Team

by Kenneth Brady

"We'll never give up,
we'll never give in,
until we crush you,
win, win, win!"

The cheer echoed through the bus radio's tinny speakers, followed by recorded applause.

The bus full of varsity cheerleaders took a hard left and Chrissy slid to the right in her seat, bumping into Allie's dead body. Chrissy tried to stop herself from sliding, but her muscles were stiff and didn't respond; the ropes had cut off circulation to her hands and arms long ago. Allie's corpse didn't give much, just sat there, unnaturally stiff and solid, like it was seatbelted in place. Her head lay against the seatback and rested on her shoulder, a smile on her face like she'd fallen asleep amidst thoughts of sunny days and good friends. Only the dried blood trail from the corner of her mouth betrayed that image. Chrissy let out a small squeal. She waited, bit her lip and, eventually, the bus straightened out.

Coach's voice came over the P.A. system. "Keep the noise

down, girls," she said. Her voice was slow, gravelly and penetrated Chrissy's head like a hot icepick sliding through the back of her skull. It was the voice of Chrissy's dying great-aunt Ginny, her long-dead great-grandpa Howard, and, just a little bit, the pleading voice of Coach Armstrong before she'd been eviscerated on the field that first night in Portland.

How long ago had that been? How long since she'd been in her home town? Chrissy strained to see toward the front of the bus. The clock had stopped at 12:00. She could just make out Coach's eyes glowing amber in the big rearview mirror. The eyes were looking right at her. Chrissy quickly looked away.

Coach made an even harder right turn and Allie's corpse leaned left. Congealed blood stubbornly stuck her short skirt to the vinyl seat and held her body still for a few moments, then released it with a wet, sucking sound. The dead cheerleader slid slowly toward Chrissy and pressed her against the side of the bus. Her mind reeled. She remembered the game she and Allie used to play on their way to school in the bus just last year. They'd exaggerate the corners the bus made and slowly press each other as hard as they could into the other side of the seat or the aisle. The corpse pressed her that way now, slowly, almost ridiculously slowly. Allie usually always won because she was stronger. Now Allie was dead and sticking to the seat, and she still won.

But you're still alive, Allie's corpse reminded her. *It's all up to you 'cause you're our team captain now.*

Chrissy didn't want to be team captain. The team captain was responsible. The team captain would have to lead and Chrissy knew that was one thing she didn't want. Better to be dead now, while she still had a chance. She wished more than anything that she hadn't been the only virgin on the bus and the only one who could lead the team in cheer during the finals. But what could she do?

The rest of the seats in the bus were filled with dead cheerleaders. Some were Chrissy's team. The others were the remains of the six teams they'd beaten in competition. Chrissy watched dead girls flop against the windows, against each other and against their bonds. Every time Coach turned or stopped the bus was like watching crash test dummies fall limp and boneless against their seats and dashboards in those stupid health class videos about the importance of wearing your safety belt. Chrissy hated those videos, but wished she had a safety belt or anything at all that would make her feel the slightest bit safe.

Now it was up to *Chrissy* and, even though they'd been winning the competitions, she hadn't been able to keep her teammates alive. Some team captain.

Come back and save us, she silently asked Katie. *At least save me.* But, Katie was dead and the other dead cheerleaders really weren't much help, so what good would Katie serve? She wouldn't be able to do anything either. She'd be just another body, stiffening and flopping against her seatback.

Chrissy allowed her eyelids to drop. The darkness was full of monsters in skirts with pompoms for hands, but anything was better than watching corpses swaying with the tide of traffic, even the dead weight of Allie against her right side, silent and accusing.

"We might be raped,
and we might all die,
but we'll keep our spirits
high, high, high!
Go team!"

Another recorded cheer thundered through the bus. That had been from the sixth competition, their second time in Portland. They'd crisscrossed from Portland to Phoenix to Billings to San Francisco to Denver and back to Portland. It had become permanent midnight after the last. Soon, they'd arrive in Salt Lake City, assemble the team and cheer again. And she was the leader. It would probably be the same old routine, only with a different execution.

—∞—

Chrissy opened her eyes after what seemed a few hours; she'd lost track of time in the dark. The side of her face was numb where it pressed against the glass. Allie's weight was gone from her side; there had been more hard turns while she slept. Chrissy pulled away slightly from the window and looked out.

Cars zoomed by them on the interstate, headlights blazing. No one was aware that anything out of the ordinary was going on in the bus. She stared, wide-eyed, as a black Jeep rolled by with a half-dozen college frat guys in it.

They slowed, looking at the outside of the decorated bus. It was clear from the hand-painted team slogans and cheers that this was a bus full of cheerleaders. It was not clear, though, that most of the cheers were painted in blood, or that only one of the cheerleaders inside was still alive.

The college guys spotted Chrissy through the window and waved, making lewd gestures. She tried to scream, but her throat was so dry only a soft, croaking sound made it out. And the guys wouldn't have heard it anyway. They thought she was flirting with them and made jacking-off motions with their hands. Then they sped up and Chrissy could not stop hot, acidic tears from running down her cheeks.

Coach saw the guys looking in and addressed the girls again, "Let's show them what they want to see, girls." The sickly-sweet smell of composting garbage surged through the bus with her every word.

The other girls on the left side of the bus stirred, with the sound of rustling leaves, then raised their heads, opened their eyes and smiled wide-mouthed out the windows at the guys. The girls who had slit throats or smashed faces hung back from the windows a bit, so as not to scare the guys.

Chrissy screamed and banged her head on the window. The guys looked back at her; one of them even seemed to realize that maybe something was wrong. Then a girl in the middle of the bus — a pretty redheaded sophomore named Rachel — pulled her shirt up and exposed her breasts, then leaned toward the window. The guys' attention was quickly diverted. From their Jeep, they weren't able to see the caked blood splattered on Rachel's pallid nipples, or the gaping hole in her stomach. The guys waved, yelled and one even pointed a video camera at Rachel's window. Then, they drove on past the bus.

Chrissy turned her head slowly and saw Allie, eyes open, a false grin on her face, looking out at the guys and waving. Then those eyes turned on her, a dead, distant, amber glow staring deep into Chrissy's own eyes. Allie raised one stiff index finger to her lips.

"Shh," she whispered and Chrissy bit her tongue to cut off her scream.

Chrissy wondered what the outside world thought. They couldn't be oblivious to the signs: the rivers of blood, the permanent midnight, the burning cities. But still, the guys in the Jeep didn't have a clue that anything was happening and Chrissy wondered if that was just because they were frat guys, living in a world of their own. Perhaps, everyone lived in a world of their own. She found herself hoping she was wrong and it was all just a bad dream.

Then another cheer, this time from all the dead girls in the bus in chorus.

> "We will win,
> we will survive,
> even in death,
> we're still alive."

Allie's eyes closed and she flopped back to the seatback, the smile still plastered to her face. Chrissy shivered and pressed herself tighter into the corner of the seat and the window. This was the new cheer then. The new cheer in which she would have to lead the dead. She only hoped she knew what to do when it came to it.

—∞—

The bus pulled into Salt Lake at midnight. Coach stood and opened the door to the outside world. The smell of smoke and burning flesh accompanied the sounds of screaming.

"Everybody off. We're here."

The girls stood slowly, wobbly, then filed off the bus. Chrissy was the last to stand and waited until everyone else had exited, hoping she wouldn't be missed. She watched Coach's form glide down the aisle, eyes never once leaving her. Coach reached her in ten seconds, but it felt like an hour.

Coach still looked like Coach Armstrong, the slightly overweight woman who'd advised the team for over twenty years. She still had her round ears and upturned nose. She still had the funny little cleft in her chin. But Coach was no longer human, evident as much by the glow of those amber eyes and her levitating walk as by the cummerbund of entrails she wore around her waist. They were her own and she displayed them like a trophy belt.

"Up," she said. Just a simple word, but with so much power and darkness in its utterance that Chrissy could not resist for long. Her lower back strained, her legs lifted and she was standing.

"You are the hope and the life, and the most valuable person here," Coach said.

Chrissy saw a brief flash in Coach's eyes, like maybe she remembered saying that once before, when she had meant it in a different, more encouraging way. Perhaps, there was a little human left. But then, she reached out and roughly grabbed Chrissy. One freezing cold hand went for her throat and held her fast. The other hand moved up under Chrissy's skirt and fingers scratched hot at her crotch, digging acid fingernails into her skin.

"And your will is not your own. You have another purpose. Don't forget that."

Coach let go. She pulled her hand back to smell the virgin's scent, then dropped a piece of paper in front of Chrissy.

"Your new cheer," she said. "Come, our God awaits." Then, she handed Chrissy a pair of red and black pompoms made of bone and matted human hair. "The colors of blood and disease." With that, she glided from the bus.

Chrissy's head buzzed, sensations of cold and heat pulsing through her body. She'd felt it once before, the only time she'd ever been touched sexually. Her boyfriend Rob had been so hot for her just before she'd left on the bus, but she'd been too scared then and hadn't wanted to lose her virginity to him. Not then. He'd said he'd wait, but she never called him back. Then would have been so much better than now.

Now he was dead, along with everyone else in Portland. She'd never get the chance to tell him she was wrong. She was just scared then. But if the feeling she had now was an indication of what was to come, that fear she'd once had was nothing compared to now. She hated to think of what the cheer might be. She picked up the paper and walked slowly off the bus.

The stadium was lit in a bright red glow from the surrounding city's fires. She could smell the burning flesh of Salt Lake City's residents and wasn't sure if the screams were coming from the dying in the city or the dead in the stadium seats.

She looked over the field of grass, blackened in the shape of a pentagram and around the full-to-capacity stadium. Some of the crowd she could recognize as people... men. She thought that maybe some were even people she knew from home, people who'd been turned to demons as their cities burned. Others were just *things*, misshapen blobs of flesh that may have once been human, or had just as likely never been truly alive. Demons, she realized, straight out of the worst of her nightmares, and they were all male. They were screaming, cheering and quivering with anticipation. Some of them tried to press onto the field, but they were held by an invisible force, unable to pass.

Above the crowd, high definition video screens flashed to life, broadcasting the opening ceremonies. Shots of all the cities in which they'd already cheered. All of them on fire. And radiating from them, a river of molten lava sprung up along the roughly straight-line path the cheerleaders had run: southeast from Portland, Oregon to Phoenix, Arizona; then northeast to Billings, Montana; then southwest to San Francisco, California; then east to Denver, Colorado; then northwest back to Portland. A huge inverted pentagram of molten rock set the landscape ablaze. In the rough center of it all was Salt Lake City, Utah. The audience cheered.

The screens then cut to Chrissy, standing in the field, looking small and timid compared to this mass of moving flesh. The demons went wild, cheering lecherously, fighting against the shields to enter the field and take Chrissy. It was like they, too, could sense her virginity. She sucked in a deep breath of burnt air and strode to the center of the pentagram.

The other cheerleaders from the bus were assembled around the pentagram and were standing, hands on hips, facing the center. They each held similar pompoms.

When Chrissy reached the center, the other girls began their cheer.

> "We might be raped
> and we might all die,
> but we'll keep our spirits
> high, high, high!"

They walked toward the center of the pentagram, slowly, barely moving. They repeated their cheer over and over again.

Chrissy looked at the cheer. Then she read it again a few times, just to be sure she had it right. Couldn't screw this one up. She took a deep breath and yelled it out, turning her body to each of the five points of the pentagram at every two words.

> "Do you hear me screaming,
> hear me call your name?
> I'm a virgin sacrifice,
> here for you to claim."

The audience cheered and the sky around Salt Lake City glowed dark amber above the fires. The video screens flashed images from other cities. The rivers were boiling human blood and soon entrails would be raining down all over the western half of the United States.

Chrissy did the second part of the cheer, twirled her body around and around, then jumped high in the air, landing and bouncing up and down as she cheered.

> "I summon thee,
> in the midnight hour,
> to come take me,
> and regain your power."

She dropped to do the splits on the blackened ground. The demons cheered. Energy began to trickle into her body, all along her legs, up through her panties, around her hips and flowing toward her stomach. She tried to stand, but the ground held her fast.

The other cheerleaders moved more quickly toward Chrissy, keeping their dead eyes pointed toward her. They could sense the coming. Chrissy looked around and saw Coach, a wide grin plastered on her face. Was she feeling pride for her team or could she sense the energy from the ground, too?

The ground opened up, fissures following along the lines of the pentagram. The cheerleaders straddled it, spreading their legs. Huge black tentacles snaked up from the fissures and pulled the last cheerleader from each line. As the tentacles wrapped around their bodies, the girls' faces turned from surprise to pleasure. Then, each girl screamed as the tentacle tore between their legs and cleft them in two lengthwise. The demons were jumping up and down in their seats, screaming.

This was the moment when things seemed most susceptible to error. This was Chrissy's only chance and she knew that anything was better than having the tentacled nightmare that was pushing its way up from the ground be her first. Her butt was locked to the ground and the thing in the ground, the thing she summoned, was going to have her if she didn't do something. She lay back on the ground, knees in the air.

She recalled Katie's words, spoken what seemed like years ago. "It doesn't hurt. Well, okay, so it does hurt, but it's over quickly and then you don't have to worry about it, right?" Of course, Katie was dead.

Chrissy readied the cheer she hoped would save the world from destruction. The video screens zoomed in close on her. She pulled up her skirt and addressed the crowd.

"Boys," she said to the demons.

> "I've never gotten anything
> from anyone
> and I'm waiting for you all
> to show me how it's done.
> Go team!"

The horny demons needed no second call. They acted immediately and as a group. Neither the blood spraying from the severed bodies of the dead cheerleaders nor the coming of their master could match the offer of a virgin to defile. They crashed through their bonds in a sea of screaming flesh and descended on the field.

The tentacles sensed the trouble and brushed hundreds of demons into the fissures in the ground, keeping them from its prize. Those that broke past the tentacles raced to be the first to Chrissy, but were quickly attacked by other demons, greedily wanting to be the first themselves. Some settled for attacking the dead cheerleaders. Chrissy saw Allie's body thrown to the ground and set upon by two large brown demons. The tentacles continued to advance through the dead cheerleaders, rending their flesh apart and spraying them across the field.

Then, the tentacles reached Chrissy and encircled her. The demons' numbers were dwindling and she feared that none would get to her in time.

The ground shook and a huge round chunk of earth erupted in front of Chrissy. She screamed then, finally, because whatever was coming was big and it would certainly kill her, but would inflict so much pain upon her first that she'd wish she were dead a hundred times over.

But before it could get to Chrissy, a small, muscular red demon pushed its way through the throng of bodies and fell upon her. It was claws on her shoulders, rotten meat breath in her mouth and a searing hot spike inserted into her vagina. But then, it was over and the demon lay on top of her, panting.

He looked into her eyes and she returned the gaze through tears of pain. He looked familiar. Could it be?

"I'm sorry," he said. "I couldn't help myself."

"Rob?" she asked. Then, she was sure of it. He had the same eyes, the same grin. His skin was red and leathery, but it was still him.

"Aren't you glad we waited?" Rob said, just before he was torn off her and thrown aside.

Coach's mangled body stood towering above Chrissy. "I never asked more from my girls than I would give myself," she said. With that she thrust a dagger toward Chrissy.

The roar that came from underground made Chrissy sick to her stomach, made her ears ring and her teeth vibrate. It shook the ground so violently, the walls of the stadium collapsed and the ground opened in fissures all around the stadium, pulling demons and dead cheerleaders with it. The video screens shattered all at once. Coach teetered off balance, then fell back through the ground. The tentacles withdrew into the ground and the shaking stopped.

Chrissy stood, shakily, and glanced around at the fires burning through Salt Lake City. She couldn't hear a thing and her body ached everywhere at once. Her insides burned and she recalled the rape, began to let it come back into her mind. It was Rob, yet it hadn't been Rob. No matter what she told herself, she'd still been raped. Her eyes teared and her breath caught. She was surprised she had not died. Wasn't that the cruel part, that she would have to live with all this? She regarded the fissures around her. It would just take one little step and it would be over. All over.

An eerie wail came up from the ground below then rose into the air, the voices of many girls at once. Chrissy could pick out Allie's and even Katie's voice for a few seconds.

> "We're all dead,
> but you're still alive.
> You made your sacrifice,
> now you survive."

Then a giggle and the voices were gone.

Chrissy was in shock and, somewhere inside, she knew that she hadn't even begun to recognize what she'd just been through. But, she was still alive and so was the world. Changed, yes. The both of them, her and the world. She couldn't waste her second chance.

She weakly held one bloody pompom in the air and cheered:

> "Go team!"

Katherine Morel

...it is eating most of my brain activity, then I sleep the rest of the time, I get very little else done...

OH! (is this thing on?)

Thank you so much for this Academy Award. I would like to thank my mother, the minions of he who shall not be named, as well as the hungry dark that envelops this town and those countless goat girls ever attentive... ah? I can see I have run out of time and bacteria... thank you and goodnight.

"Cthulhu Sex (ahem!) —a poem—" was originally printed in issue 13, volume I

CTHULHU SEX (AHEM!)
—A POEM—
BY KATHERINE MOREL

Twas through their connection,
she passed her infection,
soon his brain cavity would be cleared.

To see her reflection,
caused him an erection,
yet something seemed the slightest bit weird.

On closer inspection,
she scratched her complexion,
so that bloody tentacles appeared.

All through that section,
inmates cried for protection,
but all were quickly eaten and smeared.

TA DAH!

Brian Knight

Fueled by a steady supply of cigarettes, black coffee and rock music, Brian Knight strives daily to disturb and horrify through his works of fiction. He has published numerous short stories and poems in the small press. He has published two novels, *Black Day* and *Feral*, and one collection, the Stoker Recommended *Dragonfly*. His work is praised by many respected writers, including the best selling author, Douglas Clegg.

Durant Haire

Durant Haire lives in North Carolina with his wife and daughter. He's been published throughout the small press. He's the editor of the anthologies *Beyond the Dust* from Flesh & Blood Press and *Spirits & Sleuths* from Catalyst Books. He's also the Fiction Editor at the professional webzine, *Twilight Showcase*. Visit his website at www.gduranthaire.com.

"Beyond" was originally printed in issue 15, volume II

BEYOND

BY BRIAN KNIGHT & DURANT HAIRE

1

When Jazz stepped into the alley, the little guy was taking a smoke break. His garbage truck, New York City logo displayed on each front quarter panel, sat idling. Its hazard lights blinked on and off, painting the shaded alley walls a feverish red. The driver, Jazz knew, would be around the corner at Bertoloni's Diner getting a coffee. It was their routine.

The little guy, Sick Tony, stood at the rear of the truck, work gloves laid beside the controls, smoking and combing his thin greasy hair. He saw Jazz coming but didn't flinch. Jazz was a big man, bald and muscled like Mr. Clean, dressed to the nines in a black suit and polished boots.

But, Sick Tony was a firecracker. He had a black belt in street fighting from the school of Fuck You and probably a gun stashed somewhere on his person. He could handle big.

Jazz smiled as he approached, hands visible at his sides.

"I've always wanted to be a garbage man," he said, sardonically. "Is it true that you get to keep the good shit that people throw away?"

Sick Tony flicked his cigarette at Jazz's feet and opened his mouth to reply, then froze, eyes popping in shock. A second later, he grunted and danced as the taser gun previously concealed in Jazz's palm lit him up. Jazz watched Tony jittering and jerking as 50,000 volts surged through his body. Jazz grinned as Tony crumpled to the ground like a boneless mass of flesh. He killed the power to his taser and retracted the electrode. Jazz preferred his .45 auto, but in the city it was better to be discreet. Sick Tony twitched and groaned on the littered alley pavement, stunned but not dead.

"You're one sick fuck." Jazz said, then swung a heavy boot into the little man's head. Sick Tony was still then, dead or unconscious. Either way it didn't matter much to Jazz.

He looked around quickly, then bent and scooped the little man from the ground. Jazz held the bastard like a bag of dog food while he worked the controls for the garbage truck's compactor. The compactor door opened with a hydraulic whine and Jazz dumped Sick Tony, the little firecracker with the pistol and a yen for young blond boys, into the trash with a satisfied grunt.

"Shit, what a smell," Jazz said and lowered the compactor. When the hydraulic whine became strained, he released the lever and saluted. There had been no screaming from within, only a meaty crunch that might have been Sick Tony's head popping like a zit under the pressure.

Jazz smiled. One less worthless fucker in the world, he thought.

He heard whistling from the mouth of the alley. The driver was returning. Jazz continued smiling as he disappeared into the alley.

2

The phone rang three times before Rocky answered.

"Speak." His voice was low and gruff from years of smoking.

"You should turn on the news," Jazz said, matter-of-factly. "There's some good stuff on tonight."

"I saw," he said. "Local garbage man, convicted pedophile, Tony Fontana, found crushed to death in his truck. Good one."

Jazz noted the change in tone and smiled. Rocky was as tough as tough gets, a detective known on the street as someone not to be fucked with. A twenty-year veteran of the NYPD, Rocky had walked a thin line with the department for the past five years. If he weren't about to retire, they'd probably give him a desk job, or fire him. He'd cracked a few heads in his day. But, Jazz had seen a soft side in his love for the son of his estranged daughter. Not only was he a hard-ass cop, he was also a grandfather.

"How is Jacob? Have you heard from Cassie lately?"

"Last time we talked, we got into a fight about that sorry-ass boyfriend of hers. She said she was moving away with the bastard. I'll never see Jacob again."

"Sure you will. Cassie's young. She's got to get this rebellion out of her system. She'll come to her senses."

"I hope so, Jazz. I really hope so."

There were several moments of uncomfortable silence on the line before Rocky snapped out of it, remembering the business at hand.

"Your compensation is being taken care of."

"Thanks Rocky, but this one's on me," Jazz replied.

They spoke trivialities for the next few minutes. It was a readjustment period, a pause in thought for Rocky to recoup and time for Jazz to feel him out, to see if the old man had any more work for him. Jazz was almost certain there was another job and that Rocky was in turn feeling him out before he asked. Rocky knew the rules. A hit had to fit Jazz's criteria as a bona fide scumbag or it was a no go.

Finally, after a few minutes of tense silence, Rocky asked, "What's on your agenda?"

"I was thinking of Hawaii," Jazz said, nonchalantly. "I've always wanted to go shark fishing in the Pacific."

"How does Florida sound?" Rocky's voice was cold.

"It sounds fine. Why Florida?"

"We'll discuss it tomorrow at noon. The usual place."

3

It was a gray Saturday. The sky was bruised and angry, threatening to deluge the city with its tears. O'Kelly's Pub was practically empty when Jazz walked in. He saw Rocky sitting at a table in the back surrounded by a halo of cigarette smoke. Jazz went to the bar, ordered a couple pints and went back to meet Rocky.

"Okay Rock, who's the target this time? Who's the filth in Florida?" Jazz said, handing Rocky a beer.

"This one's going to be a little different."

"How's that?"

Rocky took a long drink. "I'm going with you."

"You're what?" Jazz looked incredulous.

"I haven't told you this, but I'm retiring in three weeks. I'm using the last of my vacation to cover the time. I'm working this one with you, Jazz."

"Are you sure that's wise?"

"Never been more sure in my life," Rocky said, grinding his Camel in the ashtray.

"Okay, I'm game if you are. Who's the target?"

Rocky finished his pint in one long gulp. "My daughter."

"Cassie?"

Rocky pulled a folder from the seat beside him and slid it across the table to Jazz.

"I had Ron tail her. He followed her to St. Augustine."

Jazz slowly flipped through the pictures. His eyes narrowed.

"Who's the Jerry Garcia look alike? He looks familiar."

"That's Aristotle Franklin, leader of a fast growing cult called The Society of Beyond."

"Yeah, how could I forget? The sick fuck was busted a few years back on child pornography charges." Jazz shook his head in disgust. "Wasn't he also convicted of murder?"

"Charged but not convicted. The slippery sonofabitch got off on a technicality. Anyway, it seems that Cassie's boyfriend is a member of this cult. I don't know if he's dangerous or just gullible, but I know Aristotle is not someone I want my daughter or my grandson to get to know. We've got to get down there and get them out of this mess."

"When do we leave?"

"Tomorrow, I've already got our tickets and reserved us a room at the Holiday Inn in St. Augustine. I told Ron to meet us there at five tomorrow evening. The last time I talked to him, his voice was shaky and he seemed very nervous. He told me he had some photos that I wouldn't believe, that he wasn't even sure he believed."

"Did he give you any clue to what it's about?"

"No. He had to make it quick. He was calling from a payphone and said that he might have been followed. I hope to God he's okay. Whatever he saw really got to him. In all the years I've known Ron, I've never heard him sound so… frightened."

4

They stepped off the plane in Jacksonville, picked up their luggage and rented a car. They took I-95 to St. Augustine. The heat was stifling. Jazz could hardly breathe. The humidity was bad enough in New York; he couldn't imagine living in this furnace.

"You ever think about what you want to do when you retire?" Rocky asked, shaking a Camel from his pack and bringing it to his lips.

Jazz was an ex-Marine. He owned a security consulting business. With all the assholes working to make the world such a wonderful place, business was good. He could retire tomorrow, but it was something he'd never really considered.

"Actually, I don't think about it. Hell, sometimes I wonder if I'll live long enough to have to worry about it."

"Shit, man, I've got visions of you as a septuagenarian Santa Claus, with kids on your lap and presents in your sack." Rocky exhaled with a laugh.

"You trying to say I'm getting fat?" Jazz chuckled. "How about you? What are you going to do in the golden years?"

"I'd like to be able to spend some time with my grandson and daughter." Rocky flipped his cigarette out the window and Jazz saw the worry on his face.

"We'll get them." Jazz said, glancing over at his friend. "It's going to be fine, Rock."

"I hope to God so, man."

Jazz squeezed the wheel. His hands were sweating, making the wheel sticky. He knew things were about to get a lot stickier when they started dealing with The Society. But he was ready; this is what he lived for.

After thirty-eight years of life, Jazz had yet to understand it. He'd tried religion, tried to believe that somewhere up in the vastness of space there sat a fair and loving God. But as he matured and contemplated the way of the world, he lost his faith. The reality of life was that there were two kinds of people: good and bad. The good people tried their best to live and let live, to lead happy and productive lives. The bad people tried their best to fuck that up. They raped and murdered the beauty and peace from life. If there was a God who witnessed life's suffering and did nothing to stop it, he was nothing more than a masochist, unworthy of worship.

Jazz was not a megalomaniac. He did what he did out of compassion. If he could save a child from a pedophile or a mother from a rapist or grandparent from a senseless murder, then his life would have meaning. If there turned out to be a Hell and his reward for saving lives was to burn, then he would gladly burn. At least he had acted instead of watching in apathy.

They pulled into the Holiday Inn in St. Augustine at 3:30, unloaded the car and checked in.

"While we wait on Ron," Jazz said, unpacking his suitcase, "I think I'll visit the local library and see if I can find any information online about The Society."

"Good idea. I'll call the police department and see what I can dig up."

Jazz reached in his wallet, pulled out a twenty and tossed it to Rocky.

"While you're on the phone, order us a pizza. My stomach is starting to talk to me."

"Another good idea. You like extra anchovies, right?"

"Don't even think about it. Fish belong in the water, not in tomato sauce."

Rocky sat on the bed chuckling as Jazz pulled the door shut behind him.

5

Jazz steered into traffic and headed for the library. He admired the city as he drove. St. Augustine was the nation's oldest city. It predated the English colonies by forty-two years. If things would've turned out differently, he might be speaking Spanish.

He had a thought, *I wonder how you say fucking human filth in Spanish.*

A livid band of storm clouds were moving in from the west. They'd already consumed the sun and now, the temperature began to fall. It looked like they were in for a turbulent night, but at least it had cooled off.

It took Jazz about fifteen minutes to get to the St. John's County library. He browsed a copy of the New York Times while he waited for a computer. Once he got one, it didn't take long to find out that The Society of Beyond liked their privacy. He found only a brief mention of them at a cult database site. They obviously didn't want open recruitment. They wanted to grow their ranks, but with choice candidates.

Jazz got back to the hotel just after 5:00. Rocky was ending a phone conversation. Jazz took a seat next to the air conditioning unit. Rocky hung up the phone, sat down at a small round table next to the wall and lit up a Camel.

"Find out anything at the library?"

Jazz leaned forward and rubbed his head. "Not a damn thing. I found a mention of them, but it didn't tell me anything I didn't already know. How 'bout you?"

"Well, I talked with Detective Hargrove from the St. Augustine P.D. I told him I was a freelance writer working on a series about cults. He didn't have a lot of info on The Society of Beyond, but what he did have was interesting. There're about two hundred members, mostly between the ages of 20 and 40. They live on a small five-acre compound on the coast southeast of the city. It seems for the most part they keep their noses clean. Their land is paid for and they pay their taxes. Most of them have jobs and seem to function as most normal people do. However, there have been a few complaints filed against them."

Thunder boomed in the distance. Wind whistled through the stairwell just down from their room.

"What kind of complaints?"

"Odd ones." Rocky replied, crushing his Camel out in a clear glass ashtray. "Hargrove told me that they don't have many neighbors, but the few who do live nearby have all complained of strange noises and odors."

"Strange in what way?"

"One of the complainants described them as 'unearthly.' He said the sounds were like sucking grunts and the stench of hundreds of dead fish. Funny thing is, when the police go to investigate, they find nothing out of the ordinary. None of them has ever reported hearing or smelling anything unusual."

"This is turning into a first class mystery," Jazz said, as he got up, parted the drapes and looked out.

Lightning illuminated the room, followed by a deep rumble that shook the large glass window.

"Speaking of mysteries, have you heard from Ron?"

"No, I haven't. I'm worried about him. He should've been here by now, called at least."

Jazz turned and grabbed his stomach.

"I don't know about you, but I'm starved. Did you call in a pizza?"

"Sure did," Rocky looked at his watch, "should be here any time now."

"I'll go down and grab us a couple of Cokes."

Jazz walked to the Coke machine just down from their room. An out-of-order sign hung on the machine, flapping in the turbulent air. Jazz cursed and had to walk to the other end of the hotel to find a drink machine. When he returned, he saw a Domino's Pizza delivery car driving off.

Finally, Jazz thought, I'm about to starve.

He opened the door and entered the room. Rocky was sitting on the end of his bed, his face pale and emotionless. He looked nauseous and unsteady. The room smelled of pepperoni and sausage. The pizza sat unopened on the table across the room. Rocky was holding a manila envelope and slowly looked up as Jazz pulled the door shut.

"You okay, Rock? Did you hear from Ron?"

"No, but the hotel manager just delivered this." Rocky held a large envelope between his thumb and forefinger like a thing diseased. "He had these forwarded to me as soon as they were developed."

"Pictures?"

"Yeah," Rocky said, looking sick.

"Do I want to see them?"

"No, you don't. I wish I had never opened it. If this is real, I'd rather not have known. Prepare yourself for something unbelievable."

6

Jazz opened the envelope and pulled out an 8x10 from the top of the stack inside. Rocky stared at the floor.

"Fuck Rocky," Jazz spat, then threw the pictures on the bed. "You could've just told me."

"Look again," Rocky said. His voice cracked a little at the command, but his face was steady.

"I can see what it is!" Jazz's face went from white to bright red. "It's fucking child porn." He turned and stormed to the door.

"Jazz, listen to me. This is not sex. And it's not just with children. They're changing all the members, at least the ones they deem worthy, into something... inhuman!"

Jazz turned, "What the fuck are you talking about?"

"I hardly believe it myself, still not sure that I can. But the pictures don't lie. You've got to look again."

Reluctantly, Jazz took the envelope from Rocky. The images made his gut cramp and the smell of the pizza threatened to make him puke. He forced himself to study the photos. Then, he saw it.

"What the fuck is that?" Jazz felt faint. He stumbled to the other bed and sat.

"That is Sick Tony."

"Bullshit," Jazz said with a violent shake of his head. "Tony is dead. I crushed the bastard in his trash truck." He pointed at the picture. "That can't be human."

"It isn't human," Rocky agreed, "but it is Sick Tony. I don't know how, but he's back from the dead."

Jazz looked at another photo. "Aristotle?"

"Yes."

"What are they?"

"I don't know," Rocky confessed. "My guess is that they're making more just like them."

"But why?"

"I don't know and don't care," Rocky fought back tears. "All I know is that we've got to get Jacob and Cassie out of there before it's too late."

Jazz shoved the pictures back into the envelope and tossed them on the table beside the pizza. He'd lost his appetite.

He contemplated it all for several quiet moments. What he had seen in those photos went beyond the intolerable perversion of child pornography or rape. The perpetrators in those photos, the late Sick Tony in the first and Aristotle in the second, others he had not looked at, were a perversion unto themselves, still recognizable, but no longer precisely human. They were something unnamable, all swollen tentacles, great onyx eyes, arms, legs and… other things… misplaced or missing.

"Was there a note with the photos? Anything about Jacob and Cassie?"

"Nothing. I can only assume that something horrible has happened to Ron. I just pray that it hasn't happened to Cassie and Jacob."

Jazz looked into the grandfather's eyes. Rocky was visibly older now than when they had met to work out the contract on Sick Tony. But, Jazz knew that Rocky had lost none of his strength. It was still there in his lined face, shining hard in his dark and tired eyes.

"If they've been converted…" Jazz paused, tortured by what he was about to say.

Rocky sat up straight and took in a deep breath. "I know. But I'll be the one to do it."

"Then, you're still in?"

Just then, the storm split the sky and rain poured down, blown in thick sheets by the wind.

"Oh yes," Rocky growled. "I can't think of a better night to drag those fucks back to whatever hell they came from."

7

Jazz beheld Aristotle's seaside estate from a distance. In the rain, it took a minute for him to jive what he saw with his sudden sense of unease, but when it came, it hit like a wave.

The front of the structure was wide, squat and spoke of simple beginnings. It had once housed a seafood processing plant — fish, crabs and lobsters — a slaughterhouse for the sea.

Environmentalists shut it down sometime in the late seventies. It had remained empty until the coming of Aristotle Franklin.

Now the building crawled with sickly vines that looked more like snakes than flora and twisting, coral-like spirals. It was those spirals that momentarily took Jazz's breath away. They reminded him of the things in those damned photos. The only part of the estate that had the true geometry of a structure was the original building. The rest of the complex looked like some giant abomination that had crawled out of the depths of the sea and mutated with the old building.

"God damn, that's ugly," Rocky said and Jazz actually saw him shudder.

Jazz made a U-turn and parked alongside the dirt road. From there, hid behind the natural landscape of a small wooded hill, they checked their weapons and prepared for hell.

The front door stood unguarded and unlocked. Warily, they stepped in and found themselves standing in a white sitting room. It was clean and tight like a doctor's waiting room. Chairs were arranged around a large glass coffee table. A fan of magazines covered its surface. A thin, mousy man entered from a door opposite the exit and hailed them.

"This way," he said, expressionless. "You're expected."

Rocky's hand hovered close to the butt of the gun hidden in his coat pocket. He looked at Jazz. Jazz nodded and they followed the Society man into a long hallway. Unlike the sitting room, the hall was pale white. It reminded Jazz of the belly of a fish, a dead fish.

"You are Cassie's father," the man said, nodding toward Rocky as he led them. "I don't know who you are," he said to Jazz, "but I don't like you."

"I'm hurt," Jazz said, but his face was serious.

"And you are?" Rocky urged.

"Jacob's guardian." He stopped, faced Rocky. "Cassie is no longer with us, I'm afraid. She has chosen another path and seen fit to abandon Jacob."

"Bullshit," Rocky said. Jazz saw his hand move a little closer to his concealed piece.

Not yet... not yet, Jazz thought.

"Believe what you wish," the Society man said with annoyance. "Fortunately, the Society has been good enough to care for the boy in his mother's absence."

"Yeah," Jazz agreed. "You're a den of fucking saints, aren't you? I understand your special love of children."

"You understand nothing," the Society man snapped.

Rocky seized the man's shoulder with a meathook hand, big fingers biting into flesh, then yanked him around.

"Enough bullshit! I want to see Jacob!" He reached inside his pocket with the other hand, but Jazz stopped him with a look.

"Release me," the Society man said, smiling at Rocky as if the pressure on his shoulder meant nothing to him. "You will see the boy soon enough."

"Where are you taking us?" Jazz asked.

"To see Aristotle. Jacob is with him now."

8

Aristotle reclined on something that looked more like a giant jellyfish than a chair, regarding them with an arrogant disinterest. Jacob sat cross-legged on the floor beside him. His face was pale and slack, his eyes glazed. He was drooling. The boy had been drugged.

Standing like a sentinel on the other side of Aristotle was a man who should not have been, Sick Tony. He looked like he'd been through a meat grinder, but he still breathed and that was too much for Jazz.

They saw Tony seeing them, saw the recognition, the intent in his eyes. It was all it took. Jazz and Rocky drew simultaneously and fired. Sick Tony's expression vanished in a cloud of blood, bone and diseased brain.

There was a terrible sucking sound from behind them, followed by an inhuman roar. They turned and found Jacob's guardian in the midst of his change. His body buckled and spasmed, mutating into one of the things from the photos. Burning lead shredded him before he could finish the change, decorated the stark whiteness of the hall with his insides.

When they turned back to Aristotle, he had already changed. He grinned at them, a serpent tongue flicking out between jagged teeth. He rose slowly and laughed — a sound like thunder and tearing flesh.

Jazz and Rocky emptied their guns into him, but Aristotle came at them still. Jacob slumped to the floor, watched them with disinterest.

"Aaaaahhhh!" Rocky screamed his rage and frustration. "Cocksucker, let's go!" He raised his empty piece above his head like a hatchet and waited.

"N'thugn dgth kaa!" Aristotle growled. A mass of tentacles caressed the space around him. They teased their way toward Rocky.

"Fuck!" Jazz cursed, dropped his gun and pulled out the taser. The bullets had failed to stop the beast that was Aristotle, but electricity worked just fine. The beast danced in agony. Its dark, slick skin began to steam. Its tentacles flayed in electric fury.

Rocky stepped back, ejected the spent clip from his piece and slapped another one in. He pulled the trigger twice, a slug through each of Aristotle's eyes. He sought out and found a grotesque appendage that appeared to be Aristotle's cock, and pulped it.

The beast shrieked and slumped to the floor.

"Got your back," Jazz said. "Let's move!"

Rocky scooped Jacob from the floor like a bundle of rags. Tears now streamed from the boy's dazed eyes.

They raced down the hallway, Jazz in the lead. The door to the lobby was in sight, their freedom at hand. But as they neared it, the walls began to shake and shift. Before they reached the door it had disappeared. The wall where the door had been now glistened and pulsed with life. All around them the hallway seemed in a state of transformation, shifting, rounding out like the inside of some hollow flesh tube.

The building trembled, like something waking from a long sleep.

9

"Dazzi... Sakanat... Ka-tu-lu!" The voice came at them from everywhere at once, and following it like a foul breath, the stench of a mountain of rotten fish. It was like being trapped in the intestines of some diseased giant.

All semblance of the hallway had disappeared. They stood midway in a large tunnel of oozing flesh and, as they watched, large pustules pushed themselves from the pulsing wall, ceiling and floor. In each of these murky, fluid-filled vesicles was a body, a body once human.

The converted members of The Society of Beyond began writhing in their pods, shrieking, straining to get at the intruders. Several of the cells closest to them were about to burst open. Jazz shook off the momentary shock, remembering that he had to get Jacob to safety, when he saw another vesicle directly in front of him. The contents of this one were human, a human he knew.

Jazz couldn't imagine why they'd spared Cassie. Perhaps, they were saving her for some hideous torture; perhaps, she couldn't be changed. At this point, none of that mattered. Cassie thrashed against the opaque walls of her cell, screaming for her father.

"Cassie!" Rocky screamed in disbelief.

Down the hall one of the pustules burst, its vile contents rising. Jazz steadied his arm, took aim and put a hole in the center of its head. It flopped backward with a pig-like squeal but did not die. The thing struggled to its feet and, when Jazz put a bullet in each of its abnormal kneecaps, it fell and dragged itself forward with clawed hands.

Another broke free closer to them and Jazz felled it too. Then, another one behind them and even Jazz's well-placed slugs could not stop them, only slow them down.

"Get her out, Rocky. We're running out of time!"

Rocky holstered his pistol and, getting a better grip on Jacob, pulled out a large butterfly knife. A flick of the wrist freed the blade and he sliced the sack from end to end. Rocky tossed the knife and pulled Cassie free of the membrane. She threw her arms around her father and Jacob, tears pouring down her cheeks.

"I love you, Dad. I'm sorry —"

"I love you too. But right now, we've got to concentrate on getting you two out of here. Take Jacob and stay close!"

More pods erupted and Jazz dropped the beasts as fast as he could, but still they came. One dropped from the ceiling and landed before them. A swipe of a tentacle laid Jazz's cheek open to the bone.

"Fucker!" He pulled the taser and made the beast dance. It was smaller than Aristotle had been, weaker. Steam boiled off its slick skin and it crumpled like paper in an angry fist.

"You got enough juice for them all?"

"Not a chance," Jazz said, a demented grin appearing on his face. He retracted the cable and let loose on another one.

"Then keep 'em busy while I make a door," Rocky replied.

Rocky retrieved his knife and found the spot where the door to the lobby had been. He plunged the blade into it, tugging downward with all his weight. The now living structure shuddered again, nearly knocking them off their feet, but the flesh of the wall parted. When Rocky stretched it open, the lobby, which was part of the real building, showed beyond. But even that ray of hope began to dim. The flesh of the wall began to mend and it took all of Rocky's strength to keep it open.

"Go, Cassie," he shouted. "Get Jacob out of here!"

She ran to the shrinking exit, but stopped, looking tearfully at her father. They shared a silent moment. Once again, a father and daughter connected by undying love.

"You take care of him now. I mean it!"

Cassie nodded grimly and stepped through. Seconds later, despite all Rocky's strength, the wall sealed itself.

"What now?" Rocky pulled his gun again and fired as more of the creatures came on. Nearly forty of them were free of their pods, with more quickly following.

"It probably won't work, but I've got an idea," Jazz said. "Follow my lead."

Jazz ran to the open wound that Rocky had pulled Cassie from. He drew his pistol and emptied the clip into it. Rocky joined in, emptying his clip. Then, Jazz fired the taser into the mangled flesh. As fast as he could, he retracted the electrodes and fired them again.

Rocky loaded a fresh clip and fought to keep the creatures at bay. Jazz fired the taser again and again. Just when he thought all was lost, he heard a tremendous sucking roar.

They lost their feet at once. The thing they were in shuddered and began whipping around violently. All of the creatures seemed to share in the thing's pain; they lay in the fleshy corridor writhing in agony. Then, with one massive spasm, the huge host creature collapsed around them. For the longest time all was darkness and there was no movement at all.

10

Jazz and Rocky awoke in the remains of the creature The Society of Beyond had lived in. It was already rotting and they emerged from the mess with little effort. The tableau left them dumbfounded.

As far as the eye could see the landscape was red desolation, a blood-tinted tundra. Around them, trees made of fleshless bone reached into the sky like skeletal hands. Above them, a black sun shined in an eternal high noon.

"Rocky, we ain't in Florida anymore."

Rock nodded. "But where are we?"

"Welcome to the Daath." It was Aristotle's voice. They turned and found him in the distance, perched atop a huge monolith. Hundreds of the grotesque beasts stood below him. Tentacles waved, bulbous onyx eyes glared.

"Pathetic humans! I do not die," Aristotle said. "I am!"

"We'll see about that," Jazz said, and popped a fresh clip into his piece. "You ready, friend?"

"I was born ready."

They stood side-by-side, smiles on their faces as the horde came on.

It was a good day to rid the world of filth, Jazz reckoned. Whatever world it was.

Lynne den Hartog

I've always loved writing. In fact, I wrote my first poem when I was three and a half. Unfortunately I wrote it on my bedroom wall, which put my parents in somewhat of a quandry. Should they be angry or proud? I guess they decided on the latter, as the words were still there ten years later when we moved house.

I presented them with a similar problem when I was first published. Their daughter was now a *bone fide* poet, but how could they boast that she wrote erotica? I decided to let them read my work.

"They're just like proper poems!" they exclaimed in real surprise. Their reaction was a common one, yet all I want to do is entertain people. I hope I've succeeded.

My poems have appeared in various publications and websites. An anthology of my poems and flashers, entitled *Butterflies of Love*, is available at www.amatory-ink.co.uk/

"Elegy in a Graveyard" was originally printed in issue 23, volume I

Elegy in a Graveyard
by Lynne den Hartog

Time worn stone, bathed in full moon's light,
An owl-call splits the lonely night.
Two figures lie, where all can see,
Lithe bodies twined in ecstasy.

A young musician plays on virgin strings
A melody that soars with wanton wings.
Pale naked skin reflecting silver glow,
Their breathing quickens as their fevers grow.

Strong fingers glide through jet black hair,
Hot gazes locked in frenzied stare,
Pure passion pooled in lust brimmed eyes,
Two cries fly high to starry skies.

Then silence reigns as wearied bodies rest,
Blonde head cradled on soft cushioning breast.
Then, looking up at her, with puzzled face,
He asks the question, "But why this place?"

She smiles and sighs and takes him by the hand
And speaks the words to make him understand.
"I'm honouring my father's final words to me,
'That man will have you over my dead body.'"

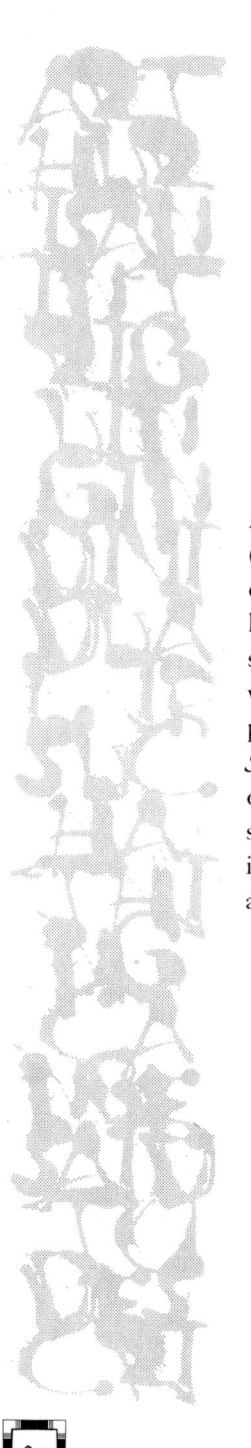

Arthur Cullipher

Arthur is an intriguing individual (if such a thing can be said to describe one such as Arthur) who has shown exceptional interest and skill in setting "stories" into the written word. We are pleased to present this work of his. *Cthulhu Sex Magazine* claims no knowledge of any connection between this story and any ongoing police investigation. We don't even know any Philips.

"A Slice of Life" was originally printed in issue 25, volume I

A Slice of Life
by Arthur Cullipher

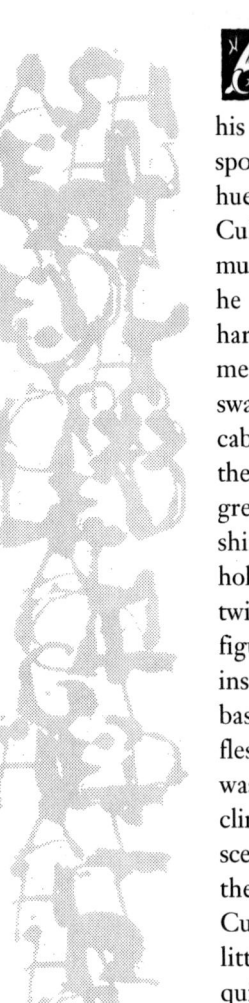

As he hobbled hurriedly along the path through his garden, gathering plump, spotted slugs and various darkly hued mushrooms into his basket, Culprit thought that the hour must surely be getting late. When he had first begun his humble harvest, a rhythmically pulsing menagerie of fireflies had been swarming about the outside of the cabin, bathing the grounds and the garden in their lovely, spastic green. But what had been a shimmering, shivering wash of hollow light faded down to only a twinkle here, a twinkle there. He figured he had best get back inside and check the clock. His basket had grown well, fat with fleshy, little, gray jewels and there was much still yet to be done. A clinging vine of early autumn rot scented the sporadic winds, aiding their chill. With his free hand, Culprit tugged his burlap cloak a little tighter around him as he quickly crept back to his shack.

A string of bones clattered and knocked one another as he thrust open the crooked, wooden door. He heard the door creaking loudly before banging shut against the frame as he read the time from the towering clock face that he had rigged into the west wall. Another rattle from the bones chimed like a cuckoo as the minute hand struck. 10:30. Good, there was still time. But he would have to work expediently and efficiently.

He set his basket on the small, scarred wood table and hung his cloak on the nail by the door. Picking an iron poker from its stand, he stoked the fire below the cauldron in the hearth. The paler tentacles surrounding his mouth writhed into a smile. His concoction was coming to a boil. He scooped up an armful of wooden doll parts from the pile stacked against the front wall of the hearth and threw them onto the fire. They caught fast as paper, burned slow as coal. Culprit drew a deep breath of their moist, tangy smoke into his lungpalps and smacked his forked tongue against the roof of his mouth. He grabbed his basket from the table and began emptying its contents into the bubbling brew, occasionally impaling particularly juicy slugs on one of his claws to suck like candy.

"Oh yes, you are a fat one, aren't you?"

From beneath the shadowed recess of the north wall, he heard tiny whimperings, but paid them little mind. He had known they had not escaped while he was in the garden. It was a good twine with which he had severed their muscles and stitched around their bones. He had braided up the whole spool from boar's mane. It was some of his best, not that they would appreciate it.

When his basket was empty, he took up the long-handled spoon and stirred. He brought a small amount of broth to his mouth, blowing away the steam before slurping it up.

"Yes, good, yes, but perhaps, eh…"

Culprit bumbled over to the cupboard. He swung the door open carelessly, causing a noisy clanging of glass to ride into the air on a dry plume of spice dust. He pointed his finger, running the long, curved nail across labels taped to jars and bottles arranged so haphazardly that it was difficult to find anything at all. Sometime soon, he thought, he really must get more organized. This whole place really needed a woman's touch.

"Ah, there you are! I found you! You tried to hide from me, didn't you? Tried to blend into the crowd, yes, but I found you! I found you!"

A healthy sprinkling of crushed molt of cicada. The powdered licorice root, a dash here, a tad there.

And parsley, yes, she likes parsley. A heaping tablespoon of parsley. Make that two. Yes.

He stirred the mixture gently, lulled by its heady aroma, preparing to taste a small sip as he heard the worn clockwork grinding away another minute. Nervously, he tapped the wooden spoon on the kettle's rim and staggered over to check the time.

10:39.

"Damn!"

Muffled screams started from the north wall at his outburst.

"Oh yes, just a minute, kiddies, just a minute. I haven't forgotten about you, don't worry, don't worry."

Culprit felt their eyes upon him as he tottered toward his hollowware cabinet. He knew they were watching him bring down the pale clay bowls he planned to set the table with, watching as he laid out placings for two. Between them, he placed a larger bowl and a sort of gravy boat, both ornately decorated in a carven frenzy of strange, enigmatically entwined worms. A couple of grimy, sloping goblets, some crooked and bent utensils, a sticky fatwax candle and a reedweave cask of violet wine crowded for the table's only remaining space.

He rustled over to a washbasin set low on the east wall, above which hung a jagged piece of filmy, gold-veined mirror. The basin was a bit rusty, being a found object like the mirror and much of the decor, even the enormous clock face. All sorts of things got lost or abandoned in these woods. All sorts. He noticed, wriggling his molish claws in the belly of the basin, that the tepid water it held had taken on an orangish hue. Lot of iron in the water out here, he thought, combing his wet, thick curled nails through his long beard of black-gold tentacles. Scratching at the paler ones beneath, he checked his features in the mirror.

It was easy to see that the landmarks of aging had taken root in his appearance. His vestigial eyes were long gone and it was plain that his skin was not as smooth or slimy as it used to be. He wet his hands again and slicked back the few hairs, thin and fine as a spider's web that sprouted from his elephantine scalp.

"My, but you are still a handsome devil, aren't you? Yes, yes I am, thank you."

Freshly groomed, Culprit made note of the time as he moved shakily to the fire. 10:45. He took the gravy boat by the handle and dipped it into the bubbling cauldron, scooping up some of its fragrant, soupy mixture. He breathed its delicious steam as he strained to reach a turkey claw from the bundle of them he had tied to the hearth's mantle. He would have to move those down. The hump on his back was becoming more pronounced these days and it was sometimes difficult to reach higher things. No time now.

The turkey's foot aerated the liquid like a whisk as he shuffled back toward the north wall.

"Well, kiddies, how do I look?"

The children stared at their captor in blank horror. He had been stuffing the plump things full of sweets and sugared fat since he had found them early yesterday evening. Cold, hungry and lost in these woods, the grubby little scoundrels had traipsed right into his house, big as you please, when Culprit was not in. But he had been delighted to see them upon his return. So much so that he had offered them his warmest hospitalities. They were frightened by his appearance, but his words were kind. When they saw that the food he offered them was wholesome and hot, undoubtedly feeling the chill fleeting from their bones, they had decided that his face was not too horrible, his twitching claws not too long or sharp.

Once they had settled in and relaxed a bit, he had even asked them their names, muttering about how lonely he was and how nice to have company. The boy, he remembered, had spoken for both his sister and himself. But, truth be told, what he said was quickly discarded from Culprit's mind. Such strange business individually naming these whiny, piggish animals. He had tried not to forget before the tincture of valerian with which he had spiked their stew carried them into its heavy embrace. Let's see. Hilda and Gerald? No, no, no. Holly and Grackel? No. Oh, uh… Handle and… no, no, that's not it either. Ah, yes, yes, I know. Kiddies.

He had taken to calling them that in their unconscious state as he strung boar's mane twine from the appropriate bones to their respective controls. Somewhat of a grueling process, really, for someone with his nervous condition. His fingernails were so long that they often got in the way of his grabbing the needle in the correct place. As a result, he had pricked his fingertips numerous times, drawing up many a dot of brass colored blood to peek out from beneath the children's thin, red fluid. Oh well, perhaps she wouldn't notice the scabs. She may even think him valiant if she did, realizing the pain he had gone through for her.

Culprit looked at the kiddies for a moment longer, wondering if they would even try to answer through their tightly gagged mouths. If he removed the gags, he knew, they would only say things like scary, ugly, gross. He saw they would be of no help after all. He would have to rely on the mirror's flattery.

The gravy grew a substantial foam as the turkey claw splashed about in it steadily and furiously. He cupped some of the thick liquid in the claw and flung it on the children. Their wide, watery eyes watched him in disbelief. He chuckled to himself, thinking about how absurd his actions must seem to them. He moved quickly, but not so much that he couldn't appreciate the spectacle of sparkling tears in the firelight, trickling down the children's cheeks and commingling with the streaked jewels of ruby-gray marinade. Beautiful, it never failed to make him sigh. Like her. Maghara. Must Hurry.

The moment he felt they had been sufficiently dowsed in his savory sauce, he shambled, stage left, toward a towering tangle of rusting gears, chipped keys, crooked pipes and bulbous stops that sprouted like groupings of unhealthy mushrooms. He called it a Malliope. It was assembled with materials gathered from a place he knew, where a traveling carnival had dumped off their damaged goods and unusables at the edges of a wide, dirt path.

It took considerable effort to loosen the crank that protruded from its side, but once set in motion, Culprit wound the instrument joyfully, faster and faster. A few pestilent notes gurglingly escaped before the thing clanked and shook to life, animate in seizure. It farted and belched thick, deformed tones that tasted hollow and acrid at their center.

The children heard a scraping rattle from behind them, like a rollercoaster starting up a hill. They felt the twine tighten around their bones. The cross-like controllers to which their appendages were strung, rolled along respective railings into the overhead position. The strings pulled taut, lifting the children a few inches from the floor of the stage, dragging them forward.

Having cranked the handle as far as he could turn it, Culprit stepped back for a moment to enjoy the show and soak in the sweet music of the Malliope. The limp bodies of the children danced violently as the twitching controls tugged and yanked at their strings. The little girl's eyes bulged comically. Her gag had grown wet and slightly yellowed with the vomit that leaked from the corners of her mouth.

Culprit read the clock. 10:52. He looked to the north wall, behind the children, for signs of change, but found only the usual wood slats. Irritated, he grumbled over to the Malliope and gave it a good, swift kick. It resonated like a diseased church bell while Culprit returned to examine the wall once more.

Yes, yes, damper now. It warped in that spot and bulged in this one. Culprit wrung his hands in anticipation, anxiously waiting for the first one to emerge. A meaty coil of wormflesh broke the surface tension of the wall. The Malliope drew them out slowly, luring them from their home with music that promised them a feast of human child flesh. Culprit jumped about, giddily clapping his hands. The Malliope's imitation of the walldwellers' song was fair and flattering for a clunking piece of machinery. He was proud of his creation.

That the walldwellers understood his pleas was sufficient enough reward. But the way they entwined their humming voices through the disjointed melody, like hungry vines weaving a strangling tapestry from which no bloom could healthily escape, swelled his frantic, inky heart with awe.

The wildly flailing children couldn't see that the wall behind them had become a wriggling cesspool, overrun with bloated serpentry, but surely they sensed the curling, ophidian presence of the many at their backsides. Culprit hoped that the constant jerking motion of the marionette controllers would keep his puppet children conscious so that they might enjoy this starving symphony, even if they couldn't feel the sniffed appraisal of their tender bodies by the frog-skinned and betentacled figures lurking beyond their sight.

Culprit turned to see the time. 10:55. Slipped through his claws, it had. Now there was a measly five minutes left to finish his preparations. The dance would have to come to a close without so much as a bow. He stomped the return pedal at the base of the Malliope and watched as the controllers rattled and dragged the convulsing puppets into the waiting mire of famished slithering.

The gagged faces of the children contorted with a pained and hopeless wonder as raspy, lamprey-toothed mouths adhered to their buttocks, hips and thighs, burrowing needled tongues into the sweet fat they found there.

The walldwellers glutted themselves ravenously, enchanted with such young meat. They drank deeply of the children's fear and confusion, even as they oiled their movements with the ruby juices of their prey. And oh, how they sang!

Culprit gathered the large bowl from the table and waited patiently for the first sprouting of his promised bounty. A fleshy bubble of palest chartreuse flowered from the slathering swarm of brilliant, eyeless gray, followed quickly by a second and a third. As he climbed onto the stage, scenes of a carnival consumed Culprit's senses. The scent of the walldwellers, like long dead meat beneath a cocoon of cotton candy from which countless maggots threaten to burst, provided such lovely accompaniment to the sickly circus tune retched from the bowels of the Malliope. Now the sight of the walldwellers' eggs, plump and rich, hanging against the writhing wall and ready to be plucked, reminded him of throwing darts at bright balloons in a small booth on the midway.

He breathed a nostalgic sigh as he began his harvest, enjoying the giving, rubbery texture of the eggs between his fingers. Perhaps he would take her to a carnival one day. Take her on all the rides, win her some prizes. Yes, she would like that.

The walldwellers had produced eleven eggs before the Malliope wound down to a rhythm too slow to hold their attention. That should be enough for the two of them and, besides, he hadn't the time to wind it again. He allowed the walldwellers to retreat, reimmersing themselves in the watery planks of the wall.

Leftover pieces of the sacrificed children plunked against the stage with a clatter like falling dominoes. Their moisture had been sapped, their remains petrified. After placing the brimming egg bowl back upon the table, slicing into a few of the more lively ones and pouring an ample amount of gravy over the delicacy, Culprit retrieved the shrunken, faux wood doll parts that the walldwellers had left. As he dumped them on the pile of others that sat by the hearth, he heard the distorted chimes of the clock striking eleven.

He looked about his cabin to ensure that everything was in order. The gong of the tolling bell droned as he excitedly uncorked the cask of violet wine and lit the fatwax candle. He shamblingly danced to the east wall for a last look in the mirror. He wet his claws once more and swiftly brushed them through his tentacles.

"Handsome, yes, handsome devil!"

The ringing of the final bell was still fading when there came a slow, heavy knock on his front door. Culprit smoothed his hair and dusted off his robes as he headed toward the sound. He paused for a moment, steadying his eager heart. He gained his composure, took a deep, calming breath and opened the door.

She stood before him stiffly beneath the light of the pale moon. It was somewhat obvious that her spine no longer fit together correctly, touching her posture with mild absurdity. Her whore's clothing was stained, tattered and garish. Her grayed skin had spots that were in need of small repair. Her eyes may have clouded, but their gaze bore the unmistakable brand of adoration. She was even lovelier now than the night they'd met.

"Ah, dearest Maghara. So nice to see you. You look absolutely stunning. Please, do come in out of the chill. There's a fire going and the table is set. I've made your favorite."

MorrisoN

Writer, Poet, Visual Artist and Professional Devil's Advocate, MorrisoN shares a NYC rat's nest with one long-suffering photographer husband, too many skittering six-legged critters, and three spooky things — two of which can be heard planning something amidst the jars of fuzzy stuff and containers of desiccated gunk all the way at the back of the 'fridge.

The other one just hides her keys a lot.

MorrisoN's Visual Art can be viddied at:
members.aol.com/exhibarts/cm.htm
and
www.wardnasse.org/3m10p.htm

"de sade begs to differ" was originally printed in issue 14, volume II

DE SADE BEGS TO DIFFER
by Morrison

staring down the shaken, quaking, sun
hell's hurricanes blasting through my veins,
burbling heart swaddled in sooty malice,
       like a black, pulsating pearl,
i sing revenge.

a sticky sweetness on the tongue,
       an enticing, juicy girl —

firm flesh fast necrotizing down to brittle white,
venom is the wine in the golden chalice,
       from which i drink and draw delight.

leviathans move through my shadows
nocturnally releasing…
anticipating what is coming
excited by what is here

nowhere to run, baby.
do you now know fear?

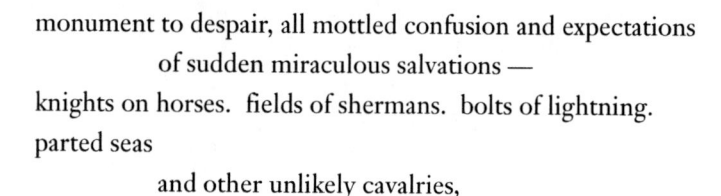

monument to despair, all mottled confusion and expectations
        of sudden miraculous salvations —
knights on horses. fields of shermans. bolts of lightning.
parted seas
        and other unlikely cavalries,

grasping frantically at straws
like scarecrow doing penance to the god of matches.
        bleating: "tomorrow,"
            while dancing down to silky ashes,

baby...
tomorrow has no place on the menu at this chez.
other succulences turn on the spit of my consideration
for the satiation of my bottom-less pit.

your vitals on the half-shell. with hollandaise.

de sade begs to differ — MorrisoN

isn't it beautiful, though, the way blood runs, oozes, slithers out

congeals to thick, luscious slugs —
        salted, sucked, savored,
            devoured and regurgitated

festive ruby ornamentations, souvenirs of secret celebrations,

rites ended in abrupt and shrieking gouts?

even god himself, i hear, is making bets, taking stock,
that regret will be the least of your worries.
caught here, as you are, with me
        and the furies,
in the writhing, sulfurous bowels of your own,
        private,
        ragnarok.

o, baby…

after i'm through tallying breadth and heft,
may he have mercy on whatever's left.

Sue D'Nimm

Sue D'Nimm is the darker half of a writer whose fiction and poetry have appeared in a wide variety of publications including *Goddess of the Bay*, *Cabal Asylum*, *Black Petals*, *The Ultimate Unknown*, *Aberrations*, *MindMares*, *The Catbird Seat*, *frisson*, *Edgar*, *Widdershins*, *Indigenous Fiction*, *Burning Sky*, and *Vampire Dan's Story Emporium* among others. D'Nimm's stories have appeared in Cara Bruce's *Viscera*, in *Delirium Magazine*, and in Shane Ryan Staley's recently published anthology, *The Dead Inn*. Her work is also posted online at venusorvixen.com and literotica.com, among many other places.

D'Nimm has been an active parapsychological researcher and has authored a book on the general topic of parapsychology. She has also worked as a teacher, business consultant and psychotherapist. She lives in Ann Arbor, Michigan.

"Romancing the Worm" was originally printed in issue 25, volume I

Romancing the Worm
by Sue D'Nimm

Little Wolf wasn't entirely sure about this Worm Woman thing. He remembered once catching a glimpse of her in the darkness of her lodge. It had happened last spring when Dancing Bear had finally emerged from his long night with her. The People said Worm Woman was as old as the red cliffs that surrounded the village and that she had no soul, having lost it on a spirit journey. With his own eyes, he had seen she had no arms or legs. Or tongue for that matter. The corn meal had dribbled from the corners of her mouth, easily escaping that vacant cavity. He remembered her eyes focusing directly on him, knowing he would be next. Her wrinkled mouth tried vainly to form words, but no sounds escaped her lips.

Dancing Bear had never been the same after that night. Despite the fact he and Little Wolf had been best friends, he had passed Little Wolf without even so much as a nod as he left Worm Woman's lodge. They had exchanged but five words since that time. Dancing Bear had even ignored Two Elks' outstretched arms, his own mother. Instead, he had gone to live in the lodge of Laughing Snake and Corn Girl, the parents of Buffalo Tooth. This was only proper, as Buffalo Tooth had been the last member of the tribe to lie with Worm Woman before Dancing Bear. Such was the way of The People.

Now, it was Little Wolf's turn. He had passed his thirteenth winter and it was now his time. To be a man of The People, he must do this thing, to lie with Worm Woman, the limbless crone-witch who harbored no soul.

Little Wolf had spent many days fasting, chewing peyote buds and courting the rattlesnake's bite. His soul had flown with the crow spirits who had taken him beyond time and space. The vision thing as an American President, whose drunken eldest son would also occupy the White House, would say a millennium from now after the White Eyes would finally get off their sorry asses and tune into the fact that the world was round.

He stood outside Worm Woman's lodge, listening to the pounding of the drums. The tune had a good beat, but it was kind of hard to dance to. Little Wolf would have given it an 86 if he were ever on Dick Clark's American Bandstand, a prospect that seemed unlikely at best, given his present circumstances.

The People stood in a circle surrounding Worm Woman's lodge, chanting Little Wolf's name, waiting for him to lift the deerskin flap and enter the old woman's lodge. He saw Dancing Bear among them. Or rather, Dancing Bear's body. He still wondered what had happened to the real Dancing Bear.

It was time. All the preparation was over. He had cleansed himself in the sweat lodge. He had smoked the Pipe of Knowing. He had kept himself pure for this very moment, unless you counted that one time with Fast Vixen behind the chokeberry bush. Horizontal mambo, here we come.

He lifted the flap. As his eyes adjusted to the darkness, he could make out the wizened face of Worm Woman. Her eyes had been gouged out, a detail he had somehow failed to notice on the last occasion — damn, The People sure loved their rituals. Her aged flesh smelled like maggots and rotting fish. Her wrinkled lips smiled in joy at the entrance of Little Wolf. He realized how truly lonely it must be for her, lying limbless in the total darkness of her lodge, patiently waiting for the next brave to pass his thirteenth winter.

Her tongueless mouth began to move and she attempted to speak.

"Awrk, awrk," she said.

Little Wolf supposed she did not get many visitors other than the braves coming to her lodge for their manhood ceremonies. She did not appear to be the greatest conversationalist in the world.

Pieces of corn meal spilled from her blistered lips as she tried to speak. The few remaining strands of her white hair were plastered to her withered cheek. Sores festered on the stumps of her amputated limbs and the odor of gangrene was in the air. Her two remaining teeth were jagged and yellow. Nice tits though.

Little Wolf tried to focus on those tits as he prepared for what he would have to do next. He shuffled over to the old crone reluctantly. He would do his part for the good old Bright Moon clan. Let no one among them say that Little Wolf was not a trooper. He would have liked to have had a paper bag to put over her head, but they wouldn't be invented for another 800 years.

Worm Woman suddenly shifted and the buffalo hides fell completely off those incongruously magnificent tits of hers. They looked almost silicone-enhanced, although Little Wolf realized that silicone would not be invented until well after paper bags. Damn those vision quests anyway. What good did it do to know what the future offered when it wouldn't come for another thousand years? Little Wolf would have to do all his silicone breast groping with ectoplasmic hands from his place among the Sky Spirits. Oh well.

Holding his nose with one hand, he reached for Worm Woman's aged flesh with the other, being careful not to stick his hand in the gangrenous spots. No sense in penetrating any more body cavities than was absolutely necessary.

He looked down at his still flaccid member. It was going to take more than the yohimbe root, horny goat weed and frog venom that The People had poured into his body in copious amounts if he were going to penetrate any body cavities at all.

Then Worm Woman's mouth began to move. She moved her jaws in a sensuous circular motion. She seemed to want him to do something. She nodded her head in the direction of Little Wolf's hitherto unresponsive organ. "Awwrp, awwrp awwrp," her tongueless mouth said in seeming explanation.

But Little Wolf thought he caught the drift of her remarks. She wanted him to surrender his genitalia to the care of her rapidly moving, nearly toothless mouth.

She knew Little Wolf needed all the help he could get.

She was also obviously extremely lonely after ten months in the darkness of her dwelling and this was going to be her big night out on the town. She wanted everything to go well. So did Little Wolf. For the sake of The People, it was important that this ceremony be concluded properly.

Grateful for whatever help he could get, Little Wolf raised his buckskin breechcloth and slowly lowered his package into Worm Woman's rapidly moving jaws.

Worm Woman grasped the skin of his scrotum in her wrinkled toothless lips at the earliest opportunity and quickly pulled Little Wolf's apparatus into her mouth's rapidly gyrating interior.

Her mouth sucked Little Wolf's right testicle in, as though it were a delicious plum just ripe for the picking. Little Wolf was soon experiencing sensations he never even imagined were possible. Who could have foreseen what hidden talents a broken stump of a tongue might harbor? Or the delights that could be made possible through the judicious nipping of a pair of decaying snaggle teeth?

Little Wolf was soon sliding up and down Worm Woman's face, his balls both completely encased in the lovely machinery of Worm Woman's mouth. The old witch certainly knew what she was doing. Not like that clueless Fast Vixen, with her endless foreplay and tentative, gentle licking of his manhood. This woman knew her way around a man's package and knew what to do with it. It was almost as though she had possessed a cock and balls of her own in some past life. There was something about a tongueless, jagged-toothed mouth that simply could not be beat.

As Wolf Woman's talented mouth mashed his balls back and forth, Little Wolf felt himself becoming completely aroused. Soon, he was as hard as a mammoth's tusk and almost as long.

He allowed Worm Woman the treat of stimulating his ass and the bottom of his balls as he slid those particular erogenous zones repeatedly over her eager lips. Little Wolf was ready and knew it was time to bring the ceremony to completion. He lifted Worm Woman's limbless body completely off the ground as he entered her. Her cunt gripped his cock as eagerly as her mouth had taken his balls. He held her magnificent tits against his chest as he slid her almost weightless body up and down his shaft. He even slipped his tongue into her mouth and was surprised to find how sensuous that hollow, two-pronged cavity could be.

The stumps of her arms bent as if to hold him as he fucked the daylights out of her limbless body. He pounded her up and down on his throbbing shaft, feeling the softness of her breasts as they slid up and down his bare chest. He felt himself start to come and began to bounce her limbless body faster and faster on his organ. Soon he felt his whole body shake and tense, as his seed spurted forth in a torrent into Worm Woman's hungrily sucking cunt. As he came, he saw a flash of lightning and was deafened by a thunderclap. Strange, he thought. He had seen no clouds before he entered Worm Woman's lodge. Soon he fell into the darkness of sleep.

—∞—

Little Wolf woke in total blackness. He felt completely satisfied. The tension that had haunted him since his recent transition through puberty was completely gone. It was almost as though he no longer had a cock and balls at all. He listened to Worm Woman's slow breathing in the darkness. That toothless crone certainly had a few tricks up her sleeve and her tongueless, limbless body carried additional advantages. This time he would not have to put up with Fast Vixen's endless prattle or her ceaseless post-coital stroking of Little Wolf's hair.

But something was wrong. The darkness was just a tad too dark. He tried to rub his eyes clear, but his hands felt too close to his shoulder to accomplish this task.

He heard his own voice admonish him, "Give it up, Little Wolf. You no longer have hands. Or eyes."

Then he realized the truth. His hands were the phantom hands that Mauled Bear raved about after he lost his arm in that skirmish with the Cheyenne. He could not see because his eye sockets were empty, their fleshy orbs having been removed and discarded long ago. He was now in the body of Worm Woman.

He heard the voice in the darkness again: "I now wear your body, Little Wolf, just as Buffalo Tooth wears mine. Such is the way it has always been. Falling Water may be this body's birth mother, but I go now to live with Two Elks, for she is the mother of my souls. In this way, The People are all of one flesh."

"Dancing Bear?" Little Wolf tried to ask, but on the first attempt the words came out sounding like "Awwrp Awwrp?" On the second attempt, he got closer: "Atnsing Air?"

"Yes, my long lost friend. I too was imprisoned in the body of Worm Woman. Just as was Buffalo Tooth before me. You now are the one to serve the People in this way. It is a great honor. Also, try doing the math. It looks like the Bright Moon clan is one body shy of a quorum. I figure the Worm Woman must have been a powerful witch and switched bodies with whatever twisted brave did this to her those many winters ago. A clever move. Poetic justice, don't you think? You've got to hand it to the old girl.

"But look on the bright side, Little Wolf. You're going to get all the corn meal you can eat without lifting a finger, so to speak. And don't worry, we won't tell the little ones, just as Buffalo Tooth never spoke to you. No sense spoiling their fun. Besides, we need to get you out of there eventually. Meanwhile, I must be going. Party time, you know. Fast Vixen awaits."

Little Wolf heard the rustle of the flap as Dancing Bear left the hut, taking Little Wolf's former body with him. His eyeless sockets regarded the total darkness in terror. Jumping Fox was only nine winters old. It would be at least three winters until he too was forced to enter Worm Woman's lodge. The gangrene suddenly hurt worse than before and the old crone's frail ticker was beating a thousand times a minute. He hoped this body would last three more winters. He had heard that corn meal was full of fiber. That was good. Wasn't it?

David Ethan Levit

Born, lived and living still — sometimes not so still, sometimes motionless. Schooled in the arcane arts of poetry at the grave of Raymond Carver by the light of Tess Gallagher, an alchemist, conjuror, white witch and enchantress. Those who fail to know her underestimate her powers. Though not entirely unharmed, David is known to have survived a griffon's claw as well as Stephen Dobyns, an executioner, dark lord and stealer-of-young-souls. With the thoughtful direction of both Mary Karr and C.D. Wright, David's path was directed through kinder hills. But it was Martha Rhodes, a saint to those lucky enough to find her, whose guidance and encouragement were no more than water and air to one who was only then half living. Finally, David would like to thank Steve Dalachinsky, a poet and a believer in poetry, without whose words, work and being, New York City would likely itself unweave.

"Thaw" was originally printed in issue 21, volume I

Thaw
by David Ethan Levit

A slow flood seeps through. Good.
        There are always cracks.

Everything is dirty, everything
        covered. Houses, people,
                they have all disappeared.

An early thaw blankets the city, and now
more than ever, the streets seem ruined.

They called it "White Hurricane."
        They called it
"Disaster," but I never trusted them.

I must explain: Some things defy music.
Like the thunder of snowflakes
        when they decay
                and crumble to their rot,
some things need to wither before they ripen.

Joi A. Brozek

Joi Brozek lives in Williamsburg, Brooklyn where she currently co-owns a bar/lounge, The Lucky Cat. "Skin" is a chapter from her first novel, *Sleeveless*, published by Phony Lid Books. Joi is currently working on her second book, *Thunderbolt*, which is a novel about love and death, freaks and rollercoasters.

"Skin" was originally printed in issue 20, volume I

SKIN

BY JOI A. BROZEK

"Designs," I say, unwilling to back down.

"No. Like, words are much cooler. They make people wonder what it might mean," says Devon.

"So do designs. And they're not as fucking obvious. Mystery, think *mystery*, girlfriend. And just remember, this little brainchild is mine. My idea."

"Fine, but I'm still doing a word. How good can a design come out anyway? Even if you *are* an artist?"

"It *will* come out fine. I just have to perfect it. Hone my craft. Don't you worry," I continue.

"If you say so, Lisha. So we're going for tomorrow afternoon?"

"Tomorrow."

We do our goodbye ritual, licking each fingertip and then touching each other's, five tips against five.

"I just know we're gonna make the other girls *die*, Lisha."

"Yeah, and you know, the day after, half of *them* will want to be sporting designs. We're going to *rule* that school."

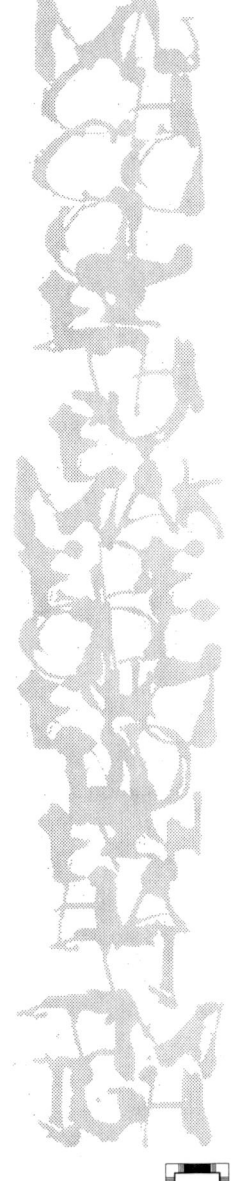

We crack up. She leaves. Devon and her silly popularity thing. I know how to play her. Devon is a nice kid, but I don't exactly need her for much. She's sort of my experiment, you know, *second in line*. She'll help spread the joy.

So, we'll see how it goes. One thing's for sure. Life at Westend School For The Arts — trends, movements, and mentalities, at least — will never be the same.

———∞———

I am standing in front of my mirror, staring at how boring I look. Staring at my pure, virgin skin. It desperately needs to be sullied, made raw and different. Thinking of the cool hologram Bandaids in the medicine cabinet. Thinking of that sharp razor blade, the corner of which stabs the heart of my ex-boyfriend, Billy, in a photo onto the cork to the right of the mirror. He looks striking that way. I take that blade and think if it is really sharp, and if my skin is as easy as the wood from which I recently carved a sculpture of an Aztec god in art class, then I've discovered yet another form of art. My high school takes pride in cultivating its students' creativity.

So, I take that blade, and make the first cut into my upper left arm. How precious, these tiny gumdrops of blood which appear immediately. I discover, after subsequent work, the blood hardly gets anywhere. It doesn't smear, unless I smudge it right away, which I don't. It doesn't even drip. It clots. Intent on a cool design, I don't waste time on getting a tissue, because I don't want to lose my creative flow. Luckily, the skin also peels into curls, much like when you drag your fingernail alongside a candle and this makes things a bit neater. Of course, this all has to be done with precision, or else maybe there could be quite a volcanic eruption of skin and blood. I file this musing for later.

I pause, thinking of road maps-bunches of squiggly lines that can often be so overwhelming. I think of my last road *trip* (if you can call it that) with my ex, done clandestinely, of course. My mother never would have gone for *that* brand of wild, hypocrite though she is. We got fucked up because I couldn't follow the damn road map. I get excited when I get lost. A cracker cop stopped me in fucking *Georgia* of all places. I must have threatened him with bodily harm, I think, because he hauled us in, called Mom and that was the end of being in temporary remission from ennui. The bloody horror! To be honest, everything happened so fast, I can't remember a this point. You know how it is when all things seem to happen at the same time. That might have been last week or last year. It's all the same to me at this point.

I keep carving. The skin surrounding the cuts is getting puffy as an indignant reaction. On the down swirl of a circle — this is not as easy as it seems — I dig in a bit too deep, so a large pearl of blood interferes and halts my precision. I blow on it and feel the sting of a paper cut-times ten maybe. Curiously, I wasn't aware of any pain before this. I get a tissue to wipe it off, but, it is like Jello and won't simply wipe off without messing the cuts. I stick my nail into this jewel and slice it off. I take that pearl of blood, and set it aside. I finish my work, which ends up looking like some sort of intricate Egyptian tribal design. But more than that. At some angles, it could even look like a impression of a road map. Like any good piece of art, there can be many different interpretations. I daresay even Dali would be proud. I have a print of his melting clocks on my bedroom wall. My nod to the Master amongst The Smiths, The Cure and Bauhaus.

But wait, I want more. There's *gotta* be more. I like the stingy feeling. I feel in *control*. Pure. Celestial. Yes, I want more. I recall the possibility of a volcano. I recall that I would never be as precise with my left hand on my right arm, because I am not yet ambidextrous. So, I slash, not as fine-tuned, I do admit, *sides* of my right wrist and arm, careful of course to avoid some major vein. Don't even think killing myself is what I am going for. I cover all of these yummy cuts, which bear a resemblance to curling ribbons, with Bandaids (I have always used a clear sparkly nail polish to cover Bandaids. It makes cuts and bruises more *festive* that way, doesn't it?).

Yes, an eruption indeed. The numb feeling tingles with my hand and I feel sloppy and out of control, so I stop. I don't like this feeling of pins and needles in my hand, and I sit, waiting for the numb to go away. I knock it against the wall to regain some other feeling.

I walk into my first class: 8:50, honors English. School's a *breeze* for me. There's Devon. She grabs an arm. She doesn't know she has grabbed a somewhat stinging spot because I am wearing long sleeves. I elbow her tit as a reflex.

"Watch what the fuck you're doing, girlfriend." I smile at her. She knows, probably because of the way I yank my arm away, like I'm trying to escape my skin.

"You..." and she stutters.

"Yeah," I answer.

"Not showing it all yet?" She's trying to insinuate that I'm scared to show it. Like I'm weak. I throw it back at her.

"I didn't feel like it yet. The designs aren't ready." She'll never win. She's nothing but a follower.

"So, will they be ready tomorrow?" she asks.

"Yeah, man, you have to let it set a day. These things can't be rushed. *Chill*."

She has no answer for that. I can see the wheels turning in her head. I don't wait for her to keep going on about it. Truthfully, the girl can be quite boring at times.

"Meet me right after school in front of the clock, Devon," I call out casually, as I go to the back of the room to sit, as far away from her as possible.

—∞—

Three p.m. and we meet.

"Lisha, I've been thinking about this all day, and, well, I thought we were in this together. Now you're a whole day ahead of me, " she whines.

"Nah. There is no 'together' in this game of pain. Be strong. Be your own person. That's what it's all about."

She looks confused.

"So, can I see?"

I show her. It was raw in the shower this morning. I guess the soap didn't help matters much, it was that Irish variety and green always seems to be the most painful color of all soaps. Not to mention the worst to have your mouth washed out with!

The blood work now looks a little more towards a shade of burgundy. It's starting to scab, as well. The pretty design is still intact on the left arm. I have been careful all night and day not to tear it by accident. Skin *is* rather delicate. I had to change to new Bandaids as well, after my shower. The black gummy rectangles surrounding the sloppy red slashes were not all that attractive.

"Nice, but I still want to do a word. I've thought about it. I'll write 'Nick.'" She looks so satisfied with herself. She wants to carve that schizo's name on herself.

"Aww, your boyfriend? Who the hell do you think you are? Sid Vicious? Get with the eighties. I still can't believe you're going out with him after what he *thinks* he does with other girls. Myself included. Ugh."

But she won't budge. *Mediocrity*, I tell you, is something I will always strive to avoid.

―∞―

We're in my room. I have every bright light turned on. I am even burning candles. The shades are down. I want a feeling of reverence to infiltrate the room. Sunlight would only ruin things. I take the blade from my ex's heart and make the first cut.

"See, now it's red and rippled like ribbons. It's *begging* and *crying* to become a design. Are you sure, *absolutely* sure, that you want to write your schizo boyfriend's name? Think of the scar. You might even be broken up by then."

"I'm sure, I'm sure. How long's it gonna take?" Her face is in a twisted grimace. I pity those strangers to pain, those who fear it. Devon's my best friend, and I *do* care. I have to prepare her.

"You know what? I'm leaving it all up to you now. You know, 'D.I.Y.'? Do it yourself. It's almost a spiritual thing. I'd be ruining it for you. I even need to leave the room, Devon."

"Ohhh. But your handwriting is better than mine," she whines.

God. I really have my work cut out for me. But I *have* to teach her to be self-reliant, even if she can't be a real artist. It's a big part of this.

"Take your time and it will come out alright. It has to be *your* thing."

And I leave. I don't even see her when she leaves my house roughly an hour later.

—∞—

Today's the day of the "opening". My debut. Devon has to wait a day, to let the cut settle, same as I did. It's important that I go first.

8:50 honors English. I make my entrance, just as the last bell rings. Last one in the door, and that's no accident. I'm wearing a tank top. Arms, sleeveless, bare and beautiful. The designs on the top of my left arm, a well-crafted design. Regal brown, now. First fierce red, then burgundy, and now brown. The haphazard whim on the right arm is still covered with Bandaids.

I hear the kids begin to buzz and the buzzing turns into the girls oohing and aahing and the boys saying things like "wicked."

I see Devon with a jealous look on her face and give her smile of serentiy. All she cares about is popularity. I'm interested in a new school order. And art for art's sake.

"Lisha, can I speak to you outside?" I hear a throat being cleared as I reach my seat. I follow Ms. Kramer out of the class.

"So, what's the deal with those slashes on your arm," she begins sardonically.

I look at my right arm where the slashes are. I am confused because they are still covered by the bandaids. Then I see her staring at my left arm. My *designs?* Slashes? I think not. I talk to her in my *I guess you're retarded* voice.

"You mean these *designs*, Mrs. Kramer? It's for art class."

"*Art class?* Who is your teacher? What kind of assignment is *that?*"

"It wasn't an *assignment*. I am not ruled by *assignments*. I am an *artist*. D.I.Y. and aberrance. That's what *art* is all about," I explain. I don't expect a mere English teacher to understand.

"Well, this is just…this is just… *beyond* me. Maybe you should go talk to Doctor Owen about this… I mean, it's not very aesthetically pleasing and you could have —"

"Oh, like I give a *damn* about your aesthetics, *honey*. That's subjective. Just like how *you* consider drivel like Anais Nin *literature*, while I'm more of a Poe gal. You dig?"

"Lisha, you're not going to pass off this…this self mutilation as *art*. When you were doing this to yourself, did you consider that you could infect yourself or even worse, cut into a major vein and *die*? Are you suicidal?

"Mrs. Kramer," I begin calmly, "I'm afraid you're projecting some psychological hang up of your own onto me. Perhaps *you* should seek the help of a shrink."

"Lisha, I'm going to have to send you to the principal. I can't allow this creative *butchering* to go unnoticed. Think of the school's reputation. You could be setting a bad example for others, too. I encourage you to tap into your creative reservoir for a new type of art."

"I think you need to get off your fat ass and go look at the school's mission statement that graces our entrance hall. I am merely expressing my creativity. It would be not only grossly unfair of you to discourage me, but also you would also be violating school policy. *I will not be censored.* I might even bring you up on discrimination charges. I will go all the way with this, I promise you that."

She is defeated. I see it in her eyes. She tries one more inane tactic.

"And what do your parents say about this," she asks weakly. Good one.

"My mother knows. *She* encourages any creative outlets." Actually, I've avoided my mother the past two days. It's not that hard. She's at church when I leave in the mornings and at her job *du jour* when I get home in the afternoons. I stay in my room all night. If I have to come in contact with her, I'll just wear sleeves.

She would be more upset about the mess I made anyway. When I really got into the volcano thing, I guess I was hacking and some skin flew all over. A few teeny pieces stuck to the mirror, even. I cleaned it all up yesterday morning. I know Jenny, who shares my room, won't tell. She worships me. Anyway, she's never around anymore so it's likely she doesn't even know about it.

"Hmm, I guess you're just too conservative for this sort of self-expression, you quixotic aging hippie. I bet the *younger* teachers will appreciate it."

"Look, Lisha, maybe there's nothing I can do about this right now. But this won't go unnoticed. It's not over."

"You have a class to teach," I remind her.

I sail into class, winner all the way. All around me, the buzzing, oohing, aahing and words.

"Lisha, cool arms. They're so pretty. Will you do mine?" I hear Ashley, most beautiful girl on campus, say. I have to think her over. She may be just a tad shallow.

"Talk to me after class."

"Pay you ten bucks."

"Later. We'll talk later. It's hard to just slap a price tag on such a thing. There are many things we need to consider."

—∞—

One week later, and there's this skin *frenzy*. I have cultivated a small distinct following of carved teens (I've transformed four others since Devon) and everyone else looks up to us and probably secretly want to be carved, too. But I am selective. I have to know their motives, for starters. Poseurs are screened the hell out by a brief interviewing process.

"If you had the chance to burn all the record albums of one rock band, which would you choose?"

(This would be almost any top 40 band, but bonus points for one of the following: Journey, Bon Jovi or Genesis.)

"Who would you kill if you could get away with it?"

(Now, if someone were to say Reagan, well, that's an automatic *in*)

"Why do you feel the need to start carving your arms?"

(There is no pat answer. I like see a variety of answers here. Of course if one lamely answers, "because it's cool," or "because I want to piss my folks off," I say, "Get the fuck out of my presence. Don't come back until you've done some soul-searching and have a less trivial motive.")

Once allowed "in", I help kids cultivate their ideas, get them started with the first cutting and then they finish the design themselves. Then, they become one of us: a Designer.

The whole school has *changed*, I tell you. There has been a static quality to the air here at Westend and I've cut through it all. Who knows what's next? I see underground ubiquity as the inevitable outcome here. They all tell me how I've changed their lives. Maybe, but it's art to me. I can't help it if they're just rejecting their weaknesses like a body does its entrails after some severe recreation gone bad. Some first-hand accounts:

"Lisha, after you left the room, and I was cutting, I felt like I was transformed onto another *plane* or something. So I carved an impression of an airplane. Thanks, Lisha."

"Lisha, I feel so in *control* of my body, now. I've even stuck to my diet and lost weight. How can I show my appreciation?" (Usually, I ask for a one time donation of fifteen bucks, for my cause and materials.)

Sure there are those who resist. I say, fine, let them discover their own thing. There are leaders, and then there are those who look for guidance. I do what I can for people. They look up to me now. I overheard one kid telling his friend that I am the unofficial guru of the entire school. All I can say is, sure pain can sometimes be a *therapeutic* art. It took someone with foresight to get people's attention. There's not a damn thing anyone can do to stop me either.

Late one afternoon Principal Flaid calls me into his office. I float in and sit directly in front of him. I'm wearing another one of my favorite tank tops. It is, after all, early June.

"Lisha, I see what Mrs. Kramer has told me yesterday is true. I was inclined to just let this sort of thing slide; we do like to encourage our students in expressing themselves in whatever form they like. I mean, several students have unconventional hair colors, boys with pierced ears even, and we have no problem with that. But in your case, well Lisha, I don't believe you realized the implications of your act. By harming yourself in such an irresponsible fashion, you have also served as the impetus for other students to follow suit. The least you could have done was keep this to yourself. Now, I have several hysterical Mothers calling me, asking what we are encouraging here. I'm afraid I'm going to have to nip this trend in the bud, or it will get really out of control. Two weeks suspension, starting tomorrow. I am sorry, but we have to set some sort of boundaries, here, or what next?"

I just nod at him. There's no point in trying to make him understand. He's trying to cover his ass. Why should I have expected anything else? Of course, I am undaunted. This isn't the end. We'll just operate subbasement. A subbasement movement lends itself to the notion of art as a perversity. I am confident that someday my vision will be realized.

"I see you are taciturn. Am I getting through to you? Art is not supposed to hurt other people. It's supposed to enlighten them, make them appreciate things they have never seen before. Things they can't even *fathom.* No, I won't pass judgment. That's not what this meeting is about. This is something for you to think about over the next two weeks."

I am inspired. I have two weeks now to do whatever I want. I smile at him, and he is confused by my reaction. He probably expected some rebellious youth. I like to catch them off-guard. Better that way, so he forgets about me and goes on to more important issues, like keeping the number of same-sex teacher affairs a secret.

I'm walking out of Flaid's office and Devon walks up to me with a shit-eating grin.

"I have two words for you Lisha, *finger digits.*"

"Say *what?*"

"The next big thing. Amputating the first digit of the finger and replacing it with a silver or gold one."

"You don't know a damn thing about art, Devon. Stick to your dancing or whatever the hell it is you do in that musty room full of graceful cookie purgers. Leave the next wave to me, *dearie.*"

Finger digits. There's no art in prosthetics. What the hell is her problem? I knew she was in it for superficial reasons.

Father Baer

A long time ago, as reckoned in the way words are counted, Father Baer was born through the squall of heated spittle onto a stony ear. Ever since this erection, he has been surrounded by the miasmal music of muses beyond memory and the baleful bleats of beasts outside belief. In the hour or two surrounding midnight, his waning specter may be glimpsed in crowded cafes and bustling bars. Before you approach him, be warned; he is more than the sum of his plenteous parts.

"19" was originally printed in issue 21, volume I

19

by Father Baer

The night reached out and bit him.
Her dark hair playing against his face,
Cool lips rubbing against his,
until...
the red neon flush of desire passed over him,
Warmth and wetness travel down his body
like traffic on a rainy summer's eve.
He dreams of this,
and other things
But,
most of all,
he dreams of her eyes.
Long, dark alleys filled with presence.
A presence more felt than seen,
filled with life.
When she looked at him,
gossamer wings brushed his mind,
face
and body
in succession.
He shivers.
The dream cracks as night's pond in the spring thaw of daybreak.
He awakens.
Hope rising with the morning sun.

Christine Morgan

Christine Morgan divides her writing time between horror, fantasy, erotica and children's fiction. A longtime gamer, she is the author of the MageLore and ElfLore fantasy trilogies and has contributed to various Steve Jackson Games products. Her zombie story "Dawn of the Living-Impaired" was nominated for an Origins Award and her debut horror novel, *Black Roses*, appeared in 2003. She is happily married, works the night shift in a psychiatric facility, and is the mother of a precocious and delightfully demented daughter. Visit her at www.christine-morgan.org.

"The Reaching Wall" was originally printed in issue 14, volume II

The Reaching Wall
by Christine Morgan

The vines.

Like long, strange hands with long strange fingers. Branching out and curling, twining.

Reaching.

Cindy forced herself to stare into the sink basin as she brushed her teeth. Down, down, at the smooth bowl of porcelain. Her wide, darting eyes made note of every minute detail. She studied the halo of rust stain around the chrome drain hole, the cap of the stopper, a glop of blue-white foam that had dripped from her toothbrush. Curds of soap residue were stuck in the ridged depression where the half-used bar of Ivory rested. The faucet was a silver arc spouting from between two seashell-shaped knobs with H and C embossed on them in gold.

Her eyes chanced higher, briefly catching a glimpse of the section of wall between the top of the sink and the bottom of the medicine cabinet. But, that was okay because years' worth of backsplash had dulled the paper into non-threatening faded ivory.

She finished brushing, spat, rinsed, spat again and deposited her toothbrush in another seashell, this one flattened with four holes in it, that jutted out of the wall above the faucet.

Reaching... the vines... closer, closer now!

Cindy, questing blindly toward the top of the toilet tank for her zippered make-up bag, froze in place.

"Nothing's reaching," she said and, though it was quiet, barely more than a whisper, she hadn't meant to speak out loud. It startled her so that she bumped her makeup bag and almost knocked it into the john. She grabbed it cat-quick and balanced it on the rim of the sink. The clatter of lipsticks and cosmetics masked any other sounds.

If there had been any other sounds to be heard.

Which there weren't.

With the door shut, she couldn't hear Kevin and his geeky friends downstairs arguing over their stupid game. And it sure wasn't as if she was hearing anything else, nothing like a stealthy whispering slithering sound of vines like fingers stretching out toward the back of her neck...

Her skin prickled in anticipation of that first alien touch of tendrils. She jerked her head forward — so she could see to put on her eye shadow, that was all! — and almost smacked her forehead into the glass.

Nose to nose with her own reflection, she still couldn't help seeing the blurred and wavering shapes of the vines in her peripheral vision. Even with her gaze fixed firmly on her own mirrored blue eyes, groping into her makeup bag and selecting by feel, she was aware of them.

But, they weren't moving. Weren't reaching. Weren't creeping and lifting themselves out of the yellow body of the wall, undulating toward her with sinister, slithery motions...

Concentrate, dummy, or you're going to put it on all screwy, she told herself.

Her tongue poked into the corner of her mouth as she carefully applied the shadow, then a bit of liner and mascara. Her hand kept wanting to shake as she was doing the latter, wanted to jab that bristly black spider-leg into the vulnerable orbs.

She somehow got through it with unjabbed orbs and dusted on some blush to give color to her cheeks, not too much. It was the funny lighting in here that made her look so pallid despite a summer at the pool. If she let that be her guide, she'd overdo it for sure. Her hand grew steadier as she put on the lipstick. A few pumps of gel and some artful primping gave her blond hair just the right lift.

Cindy was finally satisfied. Everything was perfect. Her clothes, her hair, her makeup. Perfect. No one would be able to tell her otherwise. No one would dare laugh at her or ignore her.

It was nice to be popular. To be one of the in-crowd. Admired and envied, sought-after. The party tonight would be the final proof.

And here she was, ready in record time! It would have taken longer if she'd had to take a shower, but she'd done that at school after P.E. this morning. Showering at school was easier. She didn't have to hassle with Kevin over who got to go first. She never ran out of hot water. It certainly had nothing to do with being naked and vulnerable with only a thin sheet of white vinyl shower curtain between her and the... and the rest of the bathroom. On the weekends, she took long soaks in the tub in her mother's bathroom downstairs. Because she enjoyed it.

Cindy put her make-up bag away. She kept her gaze on the floor as she headed for the bathroom door. It was marbled-green linoleum worn paler in a path that ran from door to shower stall, commode and sink. Not great, but not as creepy as the wall.

Her elbow rubbed against something fibrous and scratchy.

Cindy gasped, jumped and hugged herself with both arms. She knew what she'd see even as she whirled to face them. Oh, yes. A snaky tangle reaching, reaching from the wall, done teasing her and ready to grab...

Nothing. Two-dimensional vines frozen in their endless climb on the patterned paper. She'd brushed against the towels hanging on the rack, that was all.

A nervous laugh escaped her. Only the towels. Come on!

Though... she had been keeping to the direct middle of the path worn in the linoleum, with her arms close at her sides because she didn't want to bump into the... into anything. With her feet dead-center, her elbow couldn't have...

It was the towels! she thought vehemently. Or maybe I can just skip the party and drive on out to Ivybrook and see if they've got a jacket I can borrow. A straitjacket! How would that look in the yearbook?

She looked squarely at the wall to prove that it was just wallpaper, just ugly vine-covered wallpaper that had probably been here in this dismal wreck of a house for thirty years.

No big deal. Mom had promised they would fix everything up once they caught up with the bills. Weren't they already planning how they'd remodel the whole house? Bye-bye vines, bye-bye horrid country blue kitchen cabinets and bye-bye that goshawful orange carpet in the master bedroom where Mom slept alone.

Cindy touched the doorknob and it came alive, rattling under her palm in sudden frantic half-turns. She uttered a short, high screech and stumbled backward.

Her outcry was echoed by someone on the other side of the door. "Cindy? Are you in there?"

Kevin. He'd been trying the door, that was all.

"Don't you knock?" she snapped.

"I thought you left," he said.

"I was about —" Her words broke off abruptly as she realized she was leaning, leaning against the wall. She'd stumbled back into it and was propped up as casually as if she was waiting for a boyfriend to cruise by and pick her up after school, leaning on those vines, right up against her!

She yelped and bounded away, grabbing for the doorknob. Locked, she'd locked it against just such an eventuality as this, her doofus brother barging in on her without knocking. On purpose, most likely, trying to catch her naked because he was a pervert, a horny kid, eighteen going on twelve.

What a charge he'd get out of it and he'd tell the rest. He probably already had made up some lie, given the way they all looked at her and grinned, then laughed together when they thought she wasn't listening.

"Cindy?" Kevin knocked.

Cindy didn't look back, in case the vines, cheated from the missed opportunity, were uncoiling toward her even now. Ready to wrap around her arms and legs, noose her neck, snare her hair, bind themselves across her mouth like a gag and pull her, pull her into the wall.

She twisted the lock and yanked the door open. The corner of it skidded across the top of her shoe, would have stubbed her toes if not for the slightly sunken dip of the floor and the way it hung less than perfectly on its hinges.

Kevin barely got out of her way as she exploded into the hall. His myopic brown eyes goggled at her from behind his thick glasses.

"You okay?" he asked. "See a spider or something?"

"I'm fine, jerkazoid! What do you want?"

"To pee, if that's all right with you," he said, in the tone of voice she really hated, the one that was half condescending and half whine. "Troy's using the one downstairs. He's got the runs."

"God! Like I needed to know that." She swept him with a scornful glare, wondering once again how in the world she'd ended up with this for a brother. And a twin at that.

Not that it showed. Kevin looked as immature as he acted, was as dark as she was blond, as pasty as she was tan. Just a stick-thin geek-boy who'd never be with the popular people.

The clock down in the living room chimed seven. The party would already be starting. Everybody who was anybody was going to be there.

Well, she'd be fashionably late. It wasn't like things could get going without her.

She hurried down to the first floor. To her left was the living room, where everybody who was nobody had turned the normally neat room into a tornado-remnant of potato chip bags, empty soda cans, books, papers, funny-shaped dice and tiny metal figures.

"Garion Winterfox does not surrender!" a porky kid named Fred said as Cindy reached the bottom step. "His honor would never permit it!"

"Yeah, but you can't take out twenty goblin henchmen by yourself." Lewis was nineteen, in college and sort of cute, yet here he was with the dweebs. "Pretend to surrender and buy us some time. We'll need Garion's sword skill to get past the Warden of the Blades."

"Garion Winterfox doesn't pretend, either!"

Cindy groaned. The losers heard her, looked and instantly got that goggle-eyed look like they'd never seen a girl up close before, least of all a pretty one in a sexy new party dress. As she hurried for the kitchen, she heard one of them laugh in a way that made her think of that baby vulture on the old Bugs Bunny cartoons.

The kitchen was dark and cool, but a long rectangle of light was thrown on the tile from the door of the small utility room that doubled as her mother's home office. The gift-wrapped item she'd purchased last week at the mall was sitting on the kitchen table next to her purse.

She picked them up and stuck her head around the corner. "Hey, Mom. I'm leaving now."

A small desk was wedged between the washer-dryer and the water heater, the shelves over it crowded with computer programming and run-your-own-business books. Her mother glanced up from the spreadsheet on the screen with a tired smile.

"Okay, honey. Have fun. Back by eleven?"

"Mom, it's Friday night. And it's Jeanette's birthday. Midnight at least, please?"

"I'd hate to make you miss out on all the fun with your new friends. All right. Midnight, twelve-thirty at the latest." Mom pushed her hair behind her ears. It was as dark as Kevin's, but there were streaks of grey that hadn't been so prominent a year ago when Dad was still with them. "I told you things would be better once school started."

"I'm sorry I was so rotten about moving," Cindy said, eyes downcast.

"It's been hard on all of us. But we'll get through it, honey. You'll see."

"Do you think... When are we going to be able to start fixing the place up?"

"If I don't pay off the dentist first, they're going to come repossess your and Kevin's teeth. And the holidays are coming. Maybe in January."

"January! But Mom —"

"Cindy, it's only three months. Unless you want new carpeting for Christmas."

"No, guess not." Wallpaper! her mind shrieked. We need new wallpaper first, who cares about the dumb old carpet?

"Besides, it's not that bad," Mom said in a tone that meant she was trying to convince herself as much as Cindy. "Not as nice as our old house, but it could be a lot worse. Is Brett picking you up?"

"He said he'd meet me there. His car's in the shop and anyway, he lives on the same block as Jeanette."

"So, when do I get to meet him? Before Prom Night, I hope."

"Nobody drags their boyfriend home to meet their mother anymore."

"Because their boyfriend has tattoos on his tongue, a ring through his eyebrow and plays drums for a band called Festering Skin Disease?"

"Mom!" Cindy laughed. "He's on the debate team! His dad's a banker! And if I don't show, he's going to think I dumped him."

She went out the back door to avoid having to face Kevin's friends again. It just figured. For her brother, the move was the best thing that had ever happened to him. He'd found an entire group into all the lame things he liked.

Cindy supposed that as far as Kevin was concerned, it was worth everything they'd had to lose in order to end up here. Even Dad...

Not that Kevin cared much about that. He and Dad had nothing in common but their last names. Dad had been athletic, a high-school baseball hero, known and loved by everyone, blond, handsome and popular.

A lot like Brett Evans. Cindy was honest enough to admit to herself that part of the reason she'd been so attracted to Brett was that he reminded her of her father, or what her father had been before the... well, before.

She got in the car, the present for Jeanette resting on the passenger seat. It had been expensive and Cindy felt a twinge of guilt when she thought of Mom working so hard to make ends meet. But it was perfect for Jeanette, exactly right for her. Just what she needed.

Pine Hill was on the other side of town. It was a neighborhood far nicer than theirs and one look would have made Mom understand why Cindy could never invite Brett over. Not until they fixed things up. There were no orange carpets in Pine Hill, no faded linoleum... no reaching walls.

Cars lined the curb for three blocks around Jeanette's house. As she drove past looking for a parking place, Cindy could hear the music of a live band and smell the hickory smoke of a barbecue. People were dancing on the big brick patio in the backyard. The pool was lit from within and looked like a huge shimmering sapphire. The party was fantastic, a fabulous evening, wonderful in every way. At least, that was how it looked from the other side of the fence, from the alley, where Cindy parked in concealing darkness.

She waited until everyone else left to give Jeanette her present, surprised her in her room with it. Jeanette was so excited that she actually screamed when it came out of the box. But she only screamed once, before Cindy helped her try it on.

It was a perfect fit.

The Reaching Wall — Christine Morgan

Red always was Jeanette's color. It went so well with her complexion and it fit her like it had been painted on.

Cindy left Pine Hill at midnight and headed for home, pulling to the side of the road to let a police car and an ambulance roar past in the oncoming lane, wondering where they were going at this hour. An accident, maybe.

She was more tired than she'd expected to be. All she wanted was to fall into bed and dream of how gorgeous Brett had looked on the dance floor. Every girl had watched him and wished she was his date.

Bed would have to wait a little longer. She'd spilled something on herself and was all sticky. Mom would already be asleep, so she would have to shower upstairs.

The house was dark and silent. Cindy went to her room and got out of her damp party clothes. She dumped them in the hamper, then wrapped herself in her robe and headed for the bathroom. Her steps faltered. Maybe she should skip it.

No, she had punch or something all over her. It was in her hair, turning the blond to auburn. It was all over her arms, clear to the elbows. She could even feel spots of it drying on her face.

She locked the bathroom door and turned on the shower, opening the tiny window high in the stall to keep the steam from filling the room.

The hissing of the spray masked any other noises... not that there were any other noises, but if there had been, the hissing of the spray would have masked them. Once she was in the stall with the water beating down on her head, she could hear nothing else.

Opening her eyes to get the shampoo from the shelf, Cindy saw a shadow twining across the thin white shower curtain. Long and sinuous. Her breathing sped up.

She firmly told herself there was nothing there. Walls didn't reach for people, didn't try to grab them, pull them back inside and keep them trapped forever. Vines didn't move unless stirred by the wind. Like the ones all over the grey stone walls at Ivybrook, for instance. Wallpaper vines never moved at all.

She poured shampoo into her cupped hand and massaged it into her hair, making a face at the clotted, mucky feel of it. Yuck. Was it fruit punch? Catsup? Barbecue sauce? Whichever it was, it made a gross swirling red whirlpool around the drain.

Cindy scrubbed and scrubbed until the lather was white and foamy, then rinsed it clear and worked in some lilac-scented conditioner. She soaped herself while the conditioner set, paying special attention to her hands and forearms. It took the stiff-bristled brush to scour the places that the red stuff had grimed in, on her knuckles and under her nails.

More redness splashed across the walls and curtain in a flood. This redness didn't rinse away. It was red light, whirling through the small window in pulses.

Very dimly and distantly, even over the sounds of the water, Cindy heard a thumping. No, a hammering, a pounding. The front door? Who'd be knocking on the front door this late? They'd wake up Mom, who needed her rest. Didn't people understand how hard it was for her to have been thrust into the role of a single mother? Not by anything so ordinary as divorce or clean as death, either.

Determined to give whoever it was a piece of her mind, Cindy stepped out of the shower and reached for a towel.

A vine braceleted her wrist.

She stared at the flat green paper band against her skin. Yes, it was paper. Flat, two-dimensional and already growing sodden as it soaked up the beads of water rolling down her arm.

The wall was moving, stirring, shifting.

Reaching.

It reached for her as she stood stunned. More and more vines peeled themselves loose with faint ripping sounds as the glue backing of the wallpaper gave way.

Cindy saw strips of another design underneath, once-cheery sunflowers turned by time and decay into hideous yellow eyes. The eyes rolled to fix on her and in them she read a terrible mindless hunger.

She tried to shriek. It came out in a high, thin wail that barely even carried to her own ears.

More vines settled onto her in streamers, wrapping her like a mummy.

Her strength returned in a sudden terror-inspired burst. She lunged for the door. The wettest of the strands tore away with sickening ease, but others pulled taut. They stopped her with her desperate hand clutching for the doorknob six inches away.

It reached... it caught... raspy tendrils around her waist, her breasts, her hips. They coiled and slithered over her like snakes. One pasted itself, its underside sticky with glue, over her mouth as she found her voice to scream. Only a muffled moan emerged.

The yellow eyes in the wall blinked. A dozen eyes, twenty, more and more as the vines... except they weren't vines anymore, were they? They were tentacles, a Medusa-snarl of writhing snakes. They ripped free with sounds that weren't so much papery as scaly, and settled onto her body.

The wall was alive and it hungered. It wanted her.

She knew what would happen next. She'd be pulled back, taken into the wall, never to be free again...

Just like Dad... locked away behind the ivy forever and ever. Behind the walls and the bars. At the mercy of the attendants. He told her how they abused him, sobbed and begged her to help before the cruelest one, the one they called Bull, could hurt him again.

The vines, the tentacles, constricted and dragged Cindy away from the door. Her wet feet skidded on the marbled-green linoleum and now it was coming alive too, seething and rising up to wrap her legs.

She saw mouths among the sunflower eyes. Mouths like suckers, slurping eagerly. The reaching wall pulled her toward the mouths. Vines were all over her, vines were doing things to her that she couldn't stand to think about. She could feel them working into her. Dry and scratchy and thick.

The one over her mouth bunched and forced itself in. She bit, tasted paper, glue and rancid sap. Spitting out a chewed wad, she found her breath and finally screamed.

A thick vine drew tight around her throat, cutting off her scream. She clawed at it, but it was slick and strong. Her fingernails couldn't rip it. Not papery. Rubbery, reeking of vinyl and mildew.

Cindy grabbed for the edge of the sink. Her hands slid on the cold porcelain. Her heel came down in a puddle and she fell.

The vine around her neck pulled chokingly tight. She heard a series of popping sounds that seemed to come from far away. The vines pulled her toward the wall. Struggling, her knee slammed into the undercurve of the sink basin.

Heavy rapid thunder banged the door. It shuddered and a long jagged splinter leaped from the inside panel.

The vines were all over her, rasping, slithering, violating. She couldn't breathe. The yellow eyes and puckered rings of mouth watching from the wall leaped out at her in silent black bursts.

The door flew open. She had a dizzying impression of people, unfamiliar men in police uniforms, her mother's horrified gape, Kevin's wide-eyed stare.

Cindy tried to cry for help but her lungs burned with acid and fire. Her mother started shrieking that she was hanging herself, they had to stop her, she was killing herself just like Andrew had tried to do.

The policemen came at her, yelling to each other. The things they said made no sense. Cut the shower curtain? Couldn't they see it was the vines, the whispering greedy vines coming from the wall?

Too late.

The reaching wall drew her into darkness.

The Reaching Wall — Christine Morgan

Julie Shiel

Julie Shiel lives in Maryland with two spoiled cats and three mischievous sugar gliders. Her work appears in various magazines and anthologies including *Brutarian*, *Flesh & Blood*, *EOTU*, *Champagne Shivers*, *Aoife's Kiss*, *Twilight Times* and many others. Her first poetry collection, aptly titled *Disturbed*, is available through Project Pulp at www.blindside.net/smallpress/read/Exclusives/Disturbed/. Her webpage is located at www.horrorseek.com/horror/julieshiel/index.html.

"Possession" was originally printed in issue 25, volume I

Possession
by Julie Shiel

His mouth pressing hard,
He shoves me up against the wall,
And I watch our reflection
In the mirror down the hall.
He pulls my hips rough to his,
Slides his hands cross my skin,
Rips the lace from my body,
His teeth catch my chin.
I feel violence rise
And draw blood from his back,
I growl in frustration
At erotic attack.
When he catches my wrists,
Lies me down on the floor,
He kisses me deep,
Leaves me gasping for more.
He subdues my resistance
With his total possession,
As I slowly submit
To familiar obsession.

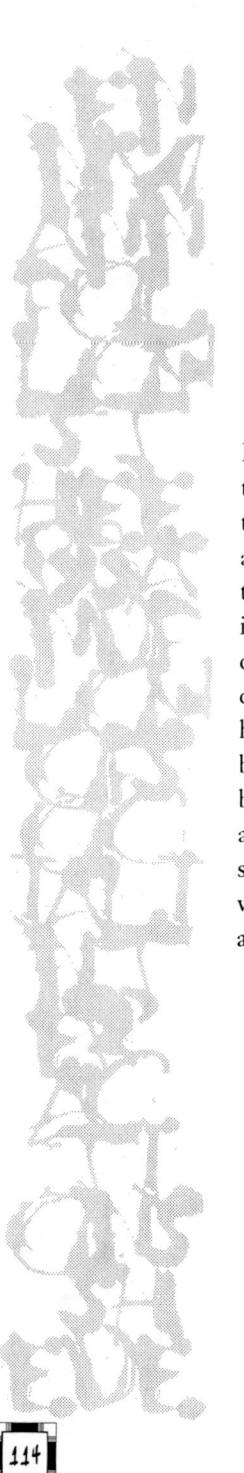

Jenn Mann

During the day, Jenn Mann, with the help of various wizards of technology, masterfully influences and controls the pitiful lives of those who cannot use their own imaginations for themselves. And during the night, she peers into the darkness between the stars for a hint of that which should not be. Between forming universes beneath her artist-beating brow and searching for the inexplicable, she enjoys curling up on the couch with a good book, a mug of coco and a warm squidimal blanket.

"The Masterpiece" was originally printed in issue 16, volume I

The Masterpiece
by Jenn Mann

Ambrosia sat before him, her heart raw from months of her hands birthing him, her hands raw from months of her heart feeding him. Now, after so much time, she sat obliviously picking at scabbed over scabs, hardened brown and burgundy skin flaking to the floor. He was her sun and she a planet pleasantly trapped in his orbit. He represented everything that she believed in: the elegant equality of strength and tenderness, the torrid marriage of goodness and evil, the lovely coexistence of ideal beauty and nightmarish grotesquery. Ambrosia stared at her seven-foot-tall creation for hours. Everything that had flowed forth from her came flooding back like hundreds of rounds of machine gun fire, each piercing her with awe.

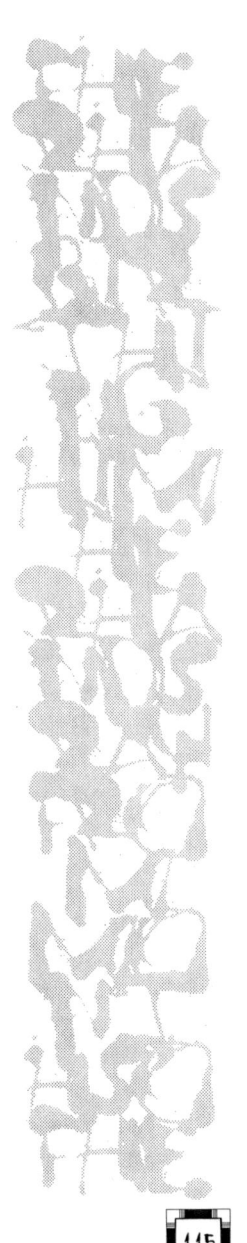

The door slammed with alarm-clock surprise, jolting Ambrosia back to reality. She slithered around the velvet curtain which designated her studio from actual living space to see that Phoenix was holding a sledgehammer in his hand and hot damp hatred in his eyes. When he saw her pale frame on that deep violet velvet background, his eyes betrayed him and transformed into brackish green puddles. It was the eyes that tore star-shaped holes through her body.

When she first met Phoenix four years earlier, his eyes sealed her fate. They looked exactly like the greenglass dragon-eyed marbles she used to play with when she was eight. Even at such a young age, she remembered thinking that the color had to have been manmade; it was too spectacular to be natural. One morning, with dew still on the tree leaves and a soupy mist in the air, she threw them up into the invisibly infinite sky only to lose them forever. They never danced on the ground again. Upon meeting Phoenix, her lime girl mind awakened and the world made more sense to her than it had in years; her marbles were staring right back at her.

Now, Ambrosia's world bore a small fissure which threatened her entire existence. Steam appeared to emanate from Phoenix's face. The intensity of his anger burning away any trace of moisture, any inkling of love, any hope of resolve. His eyes glowed dully now, with a petridish-grown-mold green. Barely green at all, really. Actually, almost grey.

"Phoenix, what's going on?" Ambrosia said, barely a whisper.

"I've had it. It's going to end tonight. I've loved you more than I thought I could love anybody and you took that love and poured it into that thing. I never saw one ounce of return from you. So to hell with you and TO HELL WITH IT!" Phoenix started towards the curtain.

"Noodooo..." Ambrosia grabbed his arm and forced him to face her.

"You don't understand, he's finished..."

"He?"

"He's finished and now there'll be more time for just you and me."

"He." Phoenix paused, seething. "Have you completely lost it? What has happened to you? I always knew you were crazy. I fell in love with your madness but you have no sense of what is real. As far as you and I go..." Phoenix took a deep breath. "Ambrosia," he said, gently touching her cheek, "there is no you and me. There hasn't been for a really long time. Too long." His arm dropped to his side as Ambrosia dropped to the floor, drowning in her own tears.

Phoenix slowly turned and entered the studio space. He stood before the sculpture, dumbfounded. The sculpture's foundation was a tree trunk, rootlike tentacles swimming out from the bottom surreptitiously surrounding (or shielding) itself. An abstract figure melted up from the base in perfect form, blooming supple, yet extremely solid arms. From these outstretched limbs sprouted serpentine branches, a universe of intravenous tubes sustaining life to a lifeless body. Each of his ten fingers miraculously birthed wings. His head, tilted back, calmly searched the ceiling for some semblance of purpose. Crevices beginning in the floor boards continued up into the creation using the human form as an irrigator of life force. His veins tabernacled within until ready to live on his own. Phoenix began to weep. Tears bounced off the sledgehammer still in hand and off his shoes to the floor, strangely disappearing as if swallowed. He collapsed with a dull thud just before the statue, creating a warped tableaux of a parishioner paying homage to a false god. Tears kept flowing and then through saltwater-blurred vision Phoenix thought he saw movement. Not trusting his judgment, he continued in his puddle of bafflement until it was too late. The wings of the sculpture fell away to reveal dagger sharp bones moving to some silent rhythm. They were soon joined by snakes and octopus tentacles which swayed in the still breeze of the apartment, leaving a strange smell of clay, forest and swamp in the air.

All Phoenix could do was wait and watch, completely overwhelmed and immobilized by fear. His heart was pounding too fast and he could feel the blood racing through his body, trying to find an escape from this horror. The bones descended on either side of his head. What were clay branches and roots twirled around him until finally stabbing into him, grabbing hold. In his final seconds, Phoenix felt all of the adoration, all of the enamourment and every last drop of love he had bestowed on Ambrosia flow back into him. His heart was full now and either didn't notice or didn't mind the fact that he was somehow being consumed by this beautiful monstrosity.

A few moments later, there was nothing left. The statue still stood but had no company. Ambrosia cautiously entered the sectioned off area. Apparently all was well except Phoenix was gone. Her eyes floated around the room, puffy from so many droplets of tears, and then she realized what had happened as if she had seen the whole thing.

"I knew there'd be more time for just you and me. Just you and me..." A slow satisfied smile crept into her countenance. She knew all she ever wanted, ever needed to do, was look at her creation, her masterpiece, with its piercing green dragon eyes and she would be happy.

The Masterpiece — Jenn Mann

William Mordore

William Mordore was born in West Cork, Ireland. He now lives in the United States.

"Wandering in the Graveyard at Night" was originally printed in issue 15, volume II

Wandering in the Graveyard at Night
by William Mordore

"I am the wanderer of graveyards
Frolicking in the black night at large

Chasing the spiritual residue
Of forgotten souls come before you

The shades of buried husbands and wives
Noble good-doers and wasted lives

That are ever moving unnoticed
Like invisible swarms of locusts

Searching for the world from whence they came
A door out of death where they remain

Writhing like thirsty fish on the land
And trampled by living feet like sand

Alas, there's no respect for the dead!"
Laments the boy to trees overhead

To weeping willows bent in sadness
To great gnarling oaks wrapped in madness

Rising from out of the hallowed ground
Where worm-riddled skulls reside year 'round

Towards the inky vastness of space
As if deformed giants lay encased

Below the blanket of mossy earth
Their arms reaching up from crawling dirt

The boy picks his way through rows of stone
Age-worn monuments of corpse's sown

Into the soil that forever thirsts
For life after the bubble has burst

Reading aloud the names of the dead
Stepping above their eternal beds

As wide-eyed owls hoot nocturnal song
Echoing throughout the shadow's throng

He kneels down in front of an old tomb
Glowing silver in light of the moon

And bows to the midnight gods of old
And the shorn sheep of the shepherd's fold

Whispers: "I heard your voices call me
O spirits of haunted memory

Like red embers in the autumn breeze
Carrying the spark of smoldered dream

As if a gale had blown them on me
And burned my skin so that I would see

The voice crying to be heard, and said
To one who would listen to the dead

Perhaps life is but one lucid daze
And death is a long unconscious maze

That has no ending; infinite road
To wander friendless and all alone

Know that I would accompany you
In limbo, for I am lonely too

So if you're listening, now is the time
To reach out to me and show a sign!"

Wandering in the Graveyard at Night — William Mordore

And shutting his eyes prepares to wait
Long inside the cemetery gates

The wind swirls dry leaves on the ground
And phantom fog creeps in all around

A black-witch cat soundlessly walks past
The meditating boy on the grass

The dark chameleon of the night
Turns once before drifting from sight

And then a noise! His heart skips a beat
To dead leaves cracking; the tread of feet!

Out of the mist a neckless head flies
An evil face with deep sunken eyes

And baggy, yellow flesh like toffee
After being chewed and all soggy

With an oozing nose that's shaped porcine
And long, sharp teeth barred like a canine

The boy's lust for death turns into fear
His rapid heart thudding in his ear

As the ghoulish face opens its mouth
And says in an angry voice, "get out!"

In a flash, he's gone, pumping his feet
Running for his dear life down the street

Leaving the ancient grave keeper there
All alone in the cool morning air

"Don't you ever come back boy, stay far!
Our ghosts are better left where they are"

Racheline Maltese

Racheline Maltese is an actor, writer and model who is grateful to no longer have a landline. She also originated the "tentacle sex" phrase that mutated into "Cthulhu Sex". You can visit her on the web at www.RachelineMaltese.com.

"The Phone Company" was originally printed in issue 13, volume I

The Phone Company
by Racheline Maltese

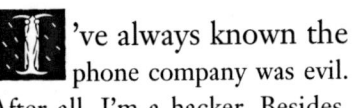

I've always known the phone company was evil. After all, I'm a hacker. Besides, they seem to think I owe them $600. So when B3n called me up at 6am on a Sunday saying he'd been playing in the tunnels again, and he had found proof of the telco's true evilness, "yeah yeah, whatever" was about all the enthusiasm I could muster. More bad wiring, or more good wiring that they claim doesn't exist, and a lot of dirt, same old, same old.

"No, really," he said. "This is serious in league with Satan sorta stuff," and then asked me to go tunneling with him the following weekend. B3n actually had a nice day job at the time, so he would only engage in activities involving dirt and potential incarceration on the weekends. I think I whined a little, made some noise about having a party to go to, but said sure. After all, I could always back out later, or unplug my phone and blame Bell Atlantic. Plus on the odd chance that B3n wasn't full of shit, a Saturday night date with Satan was definitely better than I usually managed.

Tuesday night B3n knocks me offline. I was composing my once monthly email home and hadn't bothered to turn off the call waiting. But before I even got out a greeting, I could hear B3n yammering about something. And I don't mean one of his rants about how damn cool he is, more like someone had jammed his on switch and the entire contents of his brain were going to spew out his mouth in little frothy pieces before he shut up. B3n does this sometimes. He'll stay awake for 4 days on a really horrific combo of espresso, hot chocolate and ground Vivarin.

"Dude! What're you talking about?"

His breathing was raspy.

"You having a heart attack?"

He answered by stuttering, about the phone company, about the meaning of their logo.

"Is this some sorta conspiracy theory prank? Cause if it is, I'd rather be watching X-files." I heard a train in the background. "Hey, where are you, anyway?"

He said he had to go, made me reiterate my promise to go tunneling with him on Saturday and tried to hang up, but the receiver dropped off the hook on his end and clattered against something.

I went back to emailing my mom.

Six hours later B3n called again, this time from jail. He still wasn't making a lot of sense, but his speech had at least slowed down. Dutifully, I headed downtown to relieve the jail of him and my savings account of $2,000. "Don't even talk to me until we get back to my apartment," was all I managed as a hello.

Within five seconds of walking through my door I was screaming. "What the fuck is wrong with you?!" B3n was getting pretty damn sloppy. Pretty damn weird, too. He was going from window to window pulling the shades and was making motions towards one of my phone jacks with the back of a hammer.

I managed to snatch it out of his hand a little too easily. B3n's a lot bigger than me. I leaned my back against the wall he had been about to attack and slid down it until I was crouching next to him. "What gives?" I asked real quietly. He looked confused, but I saw his shoulders start to relax. "You want a drink?"

Three hours later I had called in sick so B3n could explain what the hell was going on and drink the rest of my Bombay Sapphire while I ate Pringles and watched Jerry Springer.

The previous Sunday B3n had apparently discovered some sort of switch he had never seen before, which, it goes without saying, was pretty damn interesting. The fact that he was convinced it was alive was another matter entirely. I didn't believe him There's so much shit under New York that whatever signs of life he saw could have been rats, roaches or air currents caused by the trains. It sure as hell wasn't living fiber optics though. And it definitely wasn't growing up into my house and spying on me through the phone jack he had tried to rip out of the wall earlier. Aside from the obvious sci-fi bent of his tale, I figured, if the phone company did have living fiber optics it wouldn't have taken them eight weeks to install my line when I moved in. When I pointed this out to B3n, he responded in a monotone. "Bell Atlantic does not subscribe to logic," he said. Indeed.

After resting for a few hours we prepared for the trip. It was more than obvious B3n wasn't going to let this wait until the weekend and Jerry Springer had addled my brain enough to cause me to think that running around underground Manhattan with a guy, who was not only going insane but had a pending court case for this shit, was a good idea.

At 10pm, we walked north up the Union Square 6 platform and into the tunnel until we came to the closed off station at 18th. This was our typical staging area, as it had plenty of safe walking around room. He told me the path we were going to take, in case we got separated, and I dropped some extra gear there, to let whatever else was around know that we were too. The biggest danger underground is surprising people who don't want to be surprised.

At 20th Street we ducked west through a small archway and immediately took a metal runged ladder down, past a now closed maintenance station until we found ourselves in a half-height corridor directly below the 6 tracks. Crawling east, my claustrophobia was starting to kick in, which is why B3n was always the phone guy. The idea was to get to the never opened Second Avenue tunnels, which had been over the last twenty years co-opted by the homeless, the insane, a couple of hookers, some really bored Stuyvesant High School students and their various drug habits, and of course, the phone company, which had discovered that leaving their gear down there was safer than having it stolen out of the back of their trucks by 14-year olds who could recite the entire script of War Games.

The closed tunnels are down another level, which is part of why they were never completed. It cost too much to dig down far enough to make them safe. Once there, we headed north, instead of the usual south.

"Less people up this way," B3n said. I didn't see any at all which was pretty strange for this segment of the system. Around 34th street, the tunnel ended abruptly in an eight-foot high ladder leading literally into a crawl space. "How'd you get in there, B3n?"

"I didn't," he said. "Just poked my head in with a flashlight. Scary shit."

"Wait a second, you're telling me this drama is unfolding because of something you couldn't even get near?"

B3n turned around and grinned. "That's why I needed you."

I think I made some sort of sick noise. I could fit into that space, no question about it, but I didn't want to. "Don't worry, the room opens up, it's just the doorway that sucks," he said.

So up I went, not having much of a choice. The room in question was about five feet tall, and maybe eight by twelve.

The switch was over in the corner.

"Hey B3n, this thing is covered with water. That's bad."

"It's not water," he called back.

"Well what the fuck is it then?" I was annoyed, I could have been told all this in advance.

"I think it's mucus or something," he said.

"Dude, hand up my camera," I said crouching down and reaching my hand out. As he passed it to me I said, "Hey, I think you're just missing your sinuses a little too much and projecting on the technology."

He chuckled and popped another Vivarin.

I took off my gloves and snapped a couple of pictures, but decided to put them back on before touching the switch and its accompanying slime. There was a spark, but my gloves were insulated.

"It's just water, B3n, sparked when I tried to touch it. Water and lose wires. Bad news."

"Try to open the front panel," he said.

When I did I saw a little chattering mouth, with two-inch long, thorn-like teeth going at least 180 degrees around.

I tried to stick my screwdriver in it, but the teeth grabbed on and stopped me. I involuntarily girl screamed and immediately started trying to lower my legs out of the room.

B3n was pulling me down the ladder and banging me up pretty badly in the process.

"There's fucking teeth in there! You didn't tell me there were teeth! There's a fucking baby alligator living in there or something. I'm outta here."

I started to stalk off, but B3n stopped me, grinning again. I liked the stammering, crazy, disoriented B3n better.

"You left your camera," he sang.

"I'll buy a new one."

"I'll tell Nox what a lamer you are."

"Aren't we too old for this shit? If you wanna get bitten by some mutant alligator rat subway creature thing, go for it. I'm going home."

As I walked away, I heard B3n climb the ladder and I presume reach his hand into the room to get my camera. Then I heard scraping noises and when I turned around B3n was facing me, eyes bugging out, arm having been twisted all the way around.

Tendrils, slimy ones at that, were holding on to him, and an ever-increasing number of them were cascading out of the doorway and on to him. He held my camera in his left hand. I took a step closer and then a step back. This was bad. He looked like he was about to ask me something, when blood splattered out from the back of his head and the tooth thing burst through and replaced his own mouth. It grinned.

At this point, I just ran like hell, repeatedly banging my head on low walls. I didn't stop until I got to the 18th street platform, at which point I gathered my stuff, walked down to the Union Square station, got the hell out of the system and cabbed home.

That weekend, I took some of the hacker weenies I know to the site, to see what had happened, to see if I was going insane. B3n was still there, a bit crucified, mucoid tentacles running in and out of him. The kids thought this was the coolest thing they'd ever seen, stammering shit like "Hey, we knew you guys were '133t', but we had no idea."

B3n still clutched my camera, and the flash would go off every now and then. The mouth that wasn't his kept moving. One of the kids, Mall-lion, said, "I bet if you feed him, you'll get free phone service." I said I didn't want to get my fingers too close. I wasn't sure if the B3n I knew could hear that, but I knew he'd laugh. Mall-lion whipped out a collapsible pointer, extended it all the way and put a piece of a Snickers bar on it The little mouth went chomp and seemed happy. When it was done, the teeth started moving faster.

"Hey, we should feed it Spam!" one of the other kids shouted.

The smallest kid, and definitely the lamer of the bunch, looked at me and said, "You got a cult here, if you want it."

The kids are leading weekly trips to see B3n now, making enough money on the side to buy more used NeXt boxes. Sometimes when I go to visit him, they'll be down there, fire built in front of him, and talking Unix with each other and calling me his priestess. I laugh, but hey it's a new handle anyway. I don't, by the way, get phone bills anymore, but that could just as easily be one of the kids doing me a favor.

Sometimes, translucent pink tentacles come out of the wall B3n tried to take a hammer to. I cut them off and feed them to my cats.

Abigail Parsley

Abigail Parsley has published a number of short stories that have appeared in the zine *End of the Line*, the magazine *Cthulhu Sex*, the webzine *The Dream People* and the anthology *Tempting Disaster* among others. Despite being best known for her works that evoke a gentler feminine aspect of horror, she enjoys continuously browbeating her alter ego, Michael Amorel, into literary submission. More of her stylized works can be seen at www.michaelamorel.com.

She thanks the Goddess for her lovely son.

"He" was originally printed in issue 14, volume I

HE
BY ABIGAIL PARSLEY

Nightingale kept half his heart. He gave it willingly, innocently thinking it was all he had to give. She loved him in kind, half for half, keeping her other half locked deep inside. Ruled by her heart's fancies, she could only share half her life with him. He unwillingly did the same, hiding his in the darkness of solitude while hers sang in the bright lights of others. Because of this split and the strife it caused, they separated. In a moment of weakness due to the unfamiliar emotional pain, he let her take everything she wanted, including the half of his heart. She ripped it bleeding from him, leaving a wound that slowly scabbed and healed, still but a half.

In time, the scab fell off and left a scar. When he felt able, he timidly gave the remaining half of his heart to the caring Dove. He hoped his heart would grow back in the fertile ground of her love. In a show of compassion, she gave him her pretty necklace in return.

She used his half heart to heal her own, insensitively wounded by another. Seeing her whole pleased him. But he could only be happy the way heartless people can, living vicariously through her.

Without his heart, all he had left was a mind strong enough to stop him from sadism, but not from masochism. The pain of losing his heart piece by piece eventually grew too great. Tired of hurting himself and afraid he might accidentally hurt her, he left.

He came to New York to escape the pain of remembering.

He awoke the second morning to discover the sun was too bright. Trying to rationalize this, he attributed it to the density of atmosphere overhead. He believed the thick atmosphere at sea level diffused the light, making it cover a greater area and therefore increase its strength. He began to wear sunglasses to compensate.

He also found Dove's necklace left a curious rash around his neck. He concluded that this was from sleeping with the necklace on, which chaffed his skin. Even though he stopped wearing the necklace to bed, the rash lingered.

A week later, he noticed that sleep evaded him. He languished indoors during the day and wandered the streets at night. He was sure the lack of a heart was to blame. The need for comfort was too great to hide, burning in his chest anytime he thought of the past, which was most of the time. He grieved the loss of his heart. One half he hated; the other he loved. Where these emotions came from, he didn't take the time to discover, deciding they were constructs of his mind.

One night, while he sat at a cafe and tried to digest a cup of coffee that refused to settle, a couple of young Americans inquired about the unruly length of his hair. He hypothesized that it had grown quite long due to the cool weather. They asked if they could cut it and produced a large and rather cruel knife. He suggested they were of a diminished mental capacity, angering them greatly. Incensed, one proceeded to try without his consent. He surprised both them and himself by calmly reaching up and grabbing his assailant's arm with such strength that the poor man's forearm shattered. The knife was discarded and, after the resounding echoes from the dual cracks of bone had ceased, an amazed silence fell. Not knowing how to rectify the upsetting situation, he fled.

Upon reaching the house he was watching for a family friend, he was confronted by two police officers who calmly tried to question him about the affair earlier in the evening. Already distraught, he broke into fits of fear and furry so terrible that the kindly officers were forced to restrain him with handcuffs to keep him from hurting himself. They escorted him to the car while they whispered about the obvious mental strain of the strange fellow. Accidentally, the officers bumped his head on the car as they helped him in. Surprised by the sudden shock of pain, he seized and became stuck in the doorway. Without thought of malice, they proceeded to force him through with their billy clubs. This gentle prodding produced discomfort and invoked an uncontrollable anger. His vision faded to black.

He came to his senses surrounded by the tattered remains of the handcuffs, the car and the two befuddled police officers. Wearing confused expressions, the officers' heads stared up from the gutter at their dismembered and discarded bodies. A new sensation gripped him as he finally let the coffee follow the course it had prophetically wanted to take at the cafe. Realizing he could no longer call the house a home, he left everything behind and attempted to lose himself in the city underground.

After an uncountable number of days, nights and blackouts spent hiding under the city, he degraded to the point where he wasn't so much aware as he was reactive. His mind seemed to have gone the way of his heart and his emaciated body looked as if it was quickly following. His hair and nails had grown, colored by the sewer refuse until they were a glittering oily black. The rash had spread across his neck where the necklaces had been and healed uncleanly, forming a scar reminiscent of that discarded memento. His flesh had become albino white due to his aversion to the sun and his consequently chosen hiding places. His loss of light, mind and heart reflected most in his darkly ringed eyes. An alien light burned behind a veil of the finest black spider-webbed lace that overlaid his original hazel green. Overall, his visage had become an outward reality of the slow and steady destruction he had experienced on the inside.

Shortly after this change, a hunger began gnawing in his belly. It wasn't a hunger he normally felt; it didn't rumble like his stomach usually did. It felt like the emptiness in the place where his heart had been, but it engulfed so much more of his body and caused so much more pain.

This hunger drove him out of the underground and into the relative brightness of the moonlit night above. The glow of electric lights from the myriad poles, buildings and cars affected his eyes like the sun of past had. People encountering him turned their eyes away from his hungry stare and many moved large distances out of their way to avoid him entirely. He again donned sunglasses, discarded when he had retreated underground, as his shield against the lights and the surreptitious glares of strangers.

In his search for something to satisfy his hunger, he found a place that pandered to the type of person most resembling him. Due to the hour he chose to reappear on the face of the earth, this place was a nightclub that played hollow and painful music, populated by people wearing black clothes and make up. He fit perfectly into the decadently and extravagantly decorated and costumed crowd. And there, he could find the substances the hunger desired to be quelled with.

The hunger led him from person to person, seeking sustenance that promised lasting comfort. He found a physically needy soul who was somehow attracted to his grisly collage of a face. After he lured her to a place where they were alone, he removed his sunglasses, revealing his haunting and strangely lit eyes. With these dangerous orbs, he gazed deeply into his victim, searching for her essences. Upon finding these, he lifted them as gently as a newborn baby and lovingly drained them into his emptiness, as if that child were made of sponge and, by wringing the child strongly with both hands, he could squeeze the ambrosia of the gods into his mouth. He feasted upon her ichors, both light and dark, contenting himself as much as possible. Then, after discarding the mangled remains, he returned to his subterranean sanctuary. But the essences didn't sate him through the day and the hunger drove him above the next night.

After a period of time spent in this cycle of feasting, he realized, with some dark and twisted remnants of his mind, that he was a creature other than what he was before. This knowledge drudged something from the same mental muck, something that became a new hunger to him. This new hunger was almost moralistic, encouraging him to end the pain and suffering he caused others by ending the pain and suffering within himself. Many times, after he had drained the being of another and felt some form of inner strength, the second hunger forced him to try to destroy what he had become. After each attempt, he would wake up with a physical pain that restrained him from venturing forth to hunt. The first hunger would build until need forced him to go into the city above to feed it despite his unbearable torment.

One evening, from the miasma in his head arose a mutilated memory, long since deranged, about his previous existence with a whole heart. The secondary hunger was vanquished temporarily by his contentment at the memory's simple purity. He began to try to remember this fleeting feeling as a way to block the hunger of self-destruction for a short time after he drained his prey. After any successes he achieved, the secondary hunger always came back to haunt him even stronger than before. The mess he would make of himself to satiate this hunger would take a large number of days to recover from. Then, the cycle would start all over again.

To return to some sort of normalcy and end the constant flux, he subconsciously decided to trace the convoluted memory and regain his heart. Actual thought, let alone true memory, was harder and harder to encourage, if not non-existent. Dealing with his mangled mess of a mind the best he could, he retraced his fading past along convoluted paths, twisting under the pressure of passing time.

Almost by happenstance, he stumbled across a small piece of paper in an unremembered apartment he had serendipitously returned to. The paper had been hidden behind a mirror that he randomly smashed his clawed hand into while in a fit of inexplicable rage. He stood in the apartment, framed by the disorganized shambles from his outburst, and looked at the paper. His corrupted blood flowed down his hand and coated the broken shards of mirror, tingeing everything a reflected greenish black. The ink marks made no sense to him. He stared blankly at the language he had forgotten how to read. Even though he had no comprehension of the words on yellowed paper, there lingered the trace of a scent that flooded memories of the hated Nightingale into his atrophied mind.

She was tracked down after a long and tedious traverse across an olfactory map leading back to his city of origin. To his benefit, she still frequented places he had shown to her in misguided fits of lust. Only thinking of her as he dimly remembered she had looked during sexual intercourse, he followed her into the night, searching for an opportunity to regain his half heart. He found his chance when she turned down a dark alleyway leading to the parking structure that housed her car. After removing his glasses, he seized the opening and pressed both hands across her neck. She struggled for air and clawed at his hands. He gazed deep into her and drained forth the whole of her being as she squirmed and twisted.

During the removal and insertion of her into him, a strange yet exhilarating thing happened. As her last gasps of protest were uttered, a red spot appeared in the middle of her chest, staining her white silk blouse. As the spot widened, soaking the cloth, it started to glow a bright crimson. The illumination flitted bright then dark, faster and faster, until it strobingly issued firefly luminescence like an exhalation of cigarette smoke. He drew this into his mouth the way an old man gasps at his inhaler. The vapors had a curious affect on him, sating the secondary hunger like no previous visions could. This was the prize he sought and he was satisfied.

He reveled in the bliss this created as it allowed him to devour victims again and again with no physical repercussions. Slowly over time, the feeling began to diminish from a jubilation of satisfaction to a passiveness of comfort. When it had subsided enough to allow the hunger of self-destruction to gain control again, he became desperate to find the final half of his heart.

The other half was much harder to find, partially due to a deeply buried part of him that continually worked at foiling any attempt. During this time, he suffered both hungers acutely, so much so that he tried to destroy himself nightly and, not succeeding, forced himself to hunt and feed even through the horror of his self-inflicted pain. Partial memories of past events revealed themselves more and more frequently in more and more frightening ways. This was the first time he believed he had felt any emotions in any way for a long, long time, even though they were only base fear and self-loathing.

After coming out and feeding on not one, but two hapless victims, he stumbled onto the trail of Dove. He recognized her apartment from the sound of a passing train that whistled in a certain pattern before crossing a certain road. Charging up the stairs to her eighth-floor apartment, he was gripped by a curious pain that stemmed from a source somewhere within his time-chilled chest. He had to pause on the seventh floor as the pain grew to intolerance. But the hunger drove him, almost crying, up the last flight to land panting on all fours in front of her door.

The door opened and she stepped out, protected only by a white terrycloth towel so plush, he could almost feel it by sight alone. He longed to touch the body beneath, to feel the soft pleasure of the flesh he had not indulged in for as long as he could remember. She recognized this dramatically different him slowly over the space of many eons. With tears of sympathy in her eyes, she reached down to take his clawed and rigorred hand. He accepted, surprised at the flood of feelings that deluged his dimly lit brain at the contact with her tear-drenched hand.

Then, the hunger began to call, commanding him to trephinate her, to consume her totally and completely. His new emotions rebelled at this desire, stopping his hand from ripping off his glasses and sealing her fate within his carnivorous void.

In his hesitation, she guided him into the apartment. Unable to get him to answer her questions in his conflicted state, she told him of her life. He barely heard as blackness began to fall over his vision once again. With the strength of his newly recovered emotions, he willed a halt to this loss of control.

She stopped talking for a brief moment, waiting for him to answer some question he hadn't heard. It was in that moment that he decided himself on an awful plan to escape from both hungers at once, without harming the one he felt so much for so suddenly. In that brief pause, he told her to do something so terrible that she stopped everything, including breathing. She sat stock still, wearing a stupefied look. Finally, she found her voice, full of sorrow greater than any he remembered he had ever felt. His newly formed emotions were painfully whipped back and forth at the sound. He wanted to let himself escape by blacking out, as he had so many times before, but the emotions refused to let the darkness come this time. Without removing his glasses, he stared into her eyes and menacingly yelled some of the foulest threats he could ever recall hearing, trying to push her into action.

In anguished disbelief, she stood as calmly as she was able and fearfully backed into the kitchen. He followed with as much restraint as he could manage, creeping like a stalking leopard. She deliberately let him slink slowly towards her as she abutted the drawers containing the silverware. Still ranting, he watched her hand stretch above these drawers to the wooden rack that held the knives used for carving. She carefully selected the most beautifully long and sharp knife she owned. As she drew it from its hole, he felt an overwhelming sense of elation at the thought that the impending completion of his request would remove the hungers entirely.

She half-heartedly plunged the knife into his chest. The stroke was too feeble to pierce the bone. Ceasing the tirade he had tormented her with, he reached up with a shaking gnarled claw and gently covered her hand with it. Together, they pushed the knife through the bone as deep as it could go, opening a course for his discolored blood to run over their hands and onto the clean white-tile floor. He stumbled and fell to his knees. At the jarring impact, his glasses slid off his face. He noticed a trace of her own red blood on her lower lip where she had uncontrollably bitten through. He felt a twinge of sorrow at the damage he had caused her, but it was quickly overcome by the physical pain riddling his body. Unable to support his falling weight, she tumbled with him. Their bodies twisted with an awkward grace a dancer would envy, to end up with his head in her lap. With eyes finally clear of lace, a smile graced his malignant face. His heart was whole once again.

Heather Highfield

Heather Highfield hails from suburban Long Island, New York. There she enjoys such wholesome recreational activities as taking in oxygen and other life-giving gases, ingesting vital nourishment, basic bipedal locomotion as well as inexplicably falling unconscious and regenerating herself for hours at a time. The following poem is the wacky brainchild of an unholy union between Heather and all the free time she shouldn't have.

Hmm.

Heather — Est. 1837

"Giant Squid" was originally printed in issue 22, volume I

GIANT SQUID!

BY HEATHER HIGHFIELD

Blue briny water swirls
It begins to take on a peculiar
Shape and consistency
Pointing out the fact
That there's something
Coming through the blue briny water

And now...

Giant squid! It will take you
Down to the deepest depths
You might drown, in fact you will
And feed the giant squid!

Watch it swim! Is it angry?
We don't know, assume it is
You might cry, in fact you will
And fear the giant squid!

Wave to your little friends
Wave goodbye and jump
Into its writhing arms
Don't wait, it saves you time
It won't help to fight
Now it's coming
Tentacles reach through briny water

Oh no...

Giant squid! Don't you worry
It will kill you right away
You're fish food, indeed you are
Respect the giant squid!

Fear its slimy tentacles
Find terror in its stare
Deploy your sperm whales and harpoons
They won't save you from the snare

That
Is
The
Giant
Squid!

Adam Falik

Adam Falik lives and writes in Brooklyn. His autobiographically flavored novel-in-progress, *Father's Day*, spans the first 185 years of a man's life. Please write to Adam at: falika@i-2000.com.

Robert Wheeler

Robert Wheeler spends much of his time upside down under the Williamsburg Bridge probing grains and patterns in which he finds living faces and things he sometimes draws or writes about. "Two Loves" includes an excerpt from *Pappy's Second Song: A Novel Sentence (and Contemporary Resubmission of Dostoyevsky's* Notes from the Underground*)*; he has been slowly compiling further biographical scraps for the continuation of *Kafka's Trial: The Higher Courts*. He can be contacted at PappysSecondSong@yahoo.com.

"Two Loves" was originally printed in issue 19, volume I

Two Loves
BY ADAM FALIK & ROBERT WHEELER

My soul cries...

one

Wearing a blue dress with long sheer sleeves and a thin line of sequins crossing her budding breasts and sharp waist, June Israel accompanied her mother, Suzanne, and new stepfather to the wedding of her mother's long-time friend, Jack. Jack had always been there, from the days of June's father, through Suzanne's multiple divorces, appearing on holidays and vacations. Jack's relationship to Suzanne was suspiciously vague. An illusion of intimacy implying greater intimacy than daylight and June's presence would allow. Throughout her childhood, adolescence, and now at the gates of her womanhood, June watched Jack with attracted attentiveness, amused and amazed by this coarse, obviously handsome man who seemed to possess free reign in the lives of June's family.

Jack was the only one of Suzanne's acquaintances who June had ever permitted familiarity. He stretched the thwarted lines of her childhood. Never buying her chocolates or holiday gifts, he taught her crude names for her anatomy, recommended she watch R-rated movies, laughed at her mother and her elegant friends, and even made fun of June's premature passion for Baroque music. He'd suggest vacations in Turkey over Florence so that June could tour the brothels of Istanbul to learn the attitude of subservience. He'd perform card tricks with decks of naked women whose eyes were censored by lines of thick black ink. He'd suggest, always with both women present, that Suzanne cease June's allowance so that June would be forced to steal from her mother's purse and learn how to cash in her Bat Mitzvah bonds. He'd invite June into the mythical monologues of his sexual escapades, into his self-deprecating humor, trading June's obvious youth and female insecurities for the place of a wayward woman who would either destroy or emancipate him, who would either love him forever or discard him as the wretch he was. All the while never looking directly into June's eyes, speaking to her with hands and gestures instead of his attention, assuming her presence instead of inviting it; which was also exactly how he treated her mother. June loved how he treated both of them with equal disdain and familiar ambivalence. With a chorus of dirty limericks and sadistic suggestions, Jack maintained his presence within the compact family.

In his discordant manner, Jack secured the bond between mother and daughter. June was never so relaxed and unantagonistic in Suzanne's company as when accompanied by Jack. This was because June hoped that Suzanne and Jack were lovers, or that they at least occasionally engaged in the acts of lovers, like note following note in a ridiculously simple melody. June regarded the possible affair with enthusiasm, maintaining for years the idea of a dangerous liaison, coming as close as she ever would to admiring her mother for its sensible and practical absurdity.

At sixteen, the proximity of the two marriages suggested strategic cruelty and formulated retaliation. June imagined Suzanne's hilariously older husband and Jack's trophy wife as sacrificial pawns in the life-long game between them. And since each of the suddenly announced engagements and rushed matrimonies occurred during a two-year stretch where Jack's absence echoed, the schematic of dueling (perhaps unrequited) lovers rang with particular brilliance.

At Jack's wedding, June considered herself invisible. Her presence was only an excuse to witness the next installment, after a solemn break, of her mother's and Jack's game. She hardly noticed the new dress Suzanne had purchased for her to wear, made no resistance to the multiple fittings and alterations to adapt the dress to her maturing figure. Though June had already performed in multiple recitals and had won half a dozen musical competitions, she considered Jack's wedding the approach of her first performance, enacted solely for her amusement and demanding none of her effort.

When the two families met following the ceremony, June was not prepared for Jack's eyes. She felt she had never seen them, had never associated blue with steel or amused wrinkles with claws. Jack greeted Suzanne with disappointing lavishness, her new husband with shocking respect. All the secrets of his demeanor were reserved for June.

June's initial fear turned to disgust as she watched Jack watching her over the course of the elaborate party in the ballroom of the Plaza Hotel. She had never before experienced true disappointment in another person. Defiant of its unaccustomed taste and odor, she followed it to its source. In Jack's uninhibited glances, she discovered her own breasts, the slope of her neck at the point where the blue dress' material swept at her shoulders. In the bathroom mirror, June studied her ass, the curve of her ankles and thighs and how the dress seemed an invitation to their touch. She began to watch herself through Jack, hardening her skin against his imagined touch.

As the curtain of the night drew to a close, her genuine disgust mingling with violent awareness, she allowed Jack to follow her into a foyer hallway outside a set of bathrooms less convenient to the party. She stopped before a mirror at the end of the hall and watched him approach from behind. As she faced him, she dug her fingernails into her palms to maintain control, to choke her tears and nervous laughter, to accept whatever it was he was going to grant her.

"How does it feel, June?"

"What? How does what feel?"

"To have become a woman?"

Not knowing what to expect, she was unprepared for what she received.

"Give me a minute and I'll show you."

He nodded and she entered the bathroom. Alone in a stall, she removed a safety pin from her small satin purse. She slipped off her blue silk underwear and stuffed it behind the toilet, then put the pin inside her and carefully opened it. She stood slowly, walked to the door holding herself with greater stillness than she had ever succeeded in maintaining on stage and found Jack waiting.

"Well?" he asked.

"Here," she said. "I'll show you." She took his hand and pulled it toward her. He flinched, showing his defeat.

"You're not my father, you know. You never were."

Unsure, following only his inebriation and slipping back into his desire, he gave her his hand, let her press it against her inner thigh, moving up under the fold of her dress until he felt her delicate hairs. He pressed against her, cupped the fold of her cunt and slipped a finger, guided by hers, inside. He pricked. She held his hand until he forced it from her and backed away, appalled. His visible disgust hurt her. Wanting to cry, she turned away.

As she vomited into the bathroom sink the open pin pierced the lip of her vagina. She fell to the floor and pulled the dress around her waist. There was more blood from where it lodged in her thigh than elsewhere. She pulled the pin from her thigh but did not immediately remove it from the pierced lip. Biting her tongue against the pain, she closed the pin, locked it and sat staring between her legs at the shining cold metal against the swollen and still bleeding lip.

It was the first time she had ever pierced herself.

two

and it was only this moment i realized, real as only now can be, every muscle strung taught, long interwoven muscles, muscle-tendon, tendon-bone, fish-line-wind of flesh enacting the chaotic pattern, the spiral fractals of creation, wrapping the love of an entire universe around me, her finger nails are the wire to my soul, darts piercing, the grip between her legs pulls me into her like a noose, like a black hole if ecstasy were inside — pronoun swap, at times i feel she is the man and i the woman, i had never made love, i had never made a thing, i struggle to make it not end, never, i never want this to end and i can seem to do it no justice whatsoever: the movement is slow but makes everything swirl, if she ripped my hair out in clumps i could feel no more and i feel her more than myself, the bed is soaked, where is my mind, it is unfair to say i have no idea where my mind is, it is on and in her, her face, her open eyes where i am swimming on a fall day, the pond is full of brown leaves, i am naked inside the cold water waking my flesh, her eyes are the water and her body is the air above that tingles when i emerge, is this the womb, the tenderness that only a mother is expected to be able to share, this is the lightning storm we expect to shatter the windows and abduct us into some abstract heaven, this is her voice asking me to remain inside ([with] her), these are her hands gently set on my shoulder as if wiping a tear — am i crying, i am most assuredly crying; this is the only example i've ever had of a flame burning inside the body, the spirit-house on fire — we are dancing and the lead is somewhere far off, the music that starts the seed (the egg) to break its shell and see the wonders of the world, i am making love with the entire universe, with myself, no, WE are making love, it's spreading like a tree out of us, the earth, and filling the room with its freshness, with its desire, to overtake the whole world with its presence, its power, its motion, its compassion and concern — the Tree of Life — why can i do her no justice — i feel her grip, her grasp taking me into her, swallowing the whole of my existence, every memory, every thought, every thing i will ever be and i am nothing but us, nothing but this movement that foreshadows the universe as if everything else is just a bad joke and this, this is the only answer — the only reality i've had, somehow hearkening my earliest memories before school though not in the crib, the adventures i had alone in the woods with that childish concentrated contentment, full of awe, full of the rocks from which i am chipping mica because it sparkles, full of the tree i am climbing, full of the wonder of the vast world around me (that turns into five acres of cut trees when i grow up), how is it this returns me to childhood, that whole giving, openness, fearlessness, dancing on the old stone wall beside an endless field, the borders, if i notice, are beyond me, this is most certainly boundless, but those moments were alone, so how is it now, closer than i have ever been to another soul, i have these feelings once again... i've read or heard somewhere that you cannot be alone unless you are whole, do we have this wholeness as a child (a bond yet remembered and retained to our other half), lose it and suddenly find it again someday and realize there was a substance to the emptiness we have been fearing all these years that we tried to pass off as other things, that has made us move from place to place, job to job, any lack of contentment (a required effect), any lack of fulfillment was this (orpheus) — mind you, these things were hardly running through my mind at the moment, just the feelings, the beginning, the seed, the overwhelming bath of emotions, the drowning, the amazement so full-blown it can't even be fathomed by either of us; nipples touching to the essence, uniting two entities, stomachs touch, first with the heat of baking clay, then with ease, with ease sliding like, like nothing else; how did it begin — all this, and i've started at the end and told you nothing, excuse my avoidance in these matters, it began with certainty, with no questions of what was to come or even how amazing it would be, though i could never have imagined (all this), it began as all love stories should, with a long awaited kiss, long imagined, we kiss like a flame trying to jump off its wick, on a thread we shift, dangle and twist without effort or attempt we are gently touching lips, feeling on the edge, barely pressing along the borders but with sparks, our lips cling, dew running down a blade of grass, moisture slowly gathers and completes a drop and now we are nipping, my tongue between her teeth and upper lip, outlining her edges, stroking her teeth, exploring her innards then i am on her neck, her ear, breathing softly on the places i've just kissed, with near-hesitance i peel off her shirt to reveal her torso, her torso, i don't know where the word came from if not from her stretching that long lean... a grapevine of tendons and layers so tightly wound this torso retains a wild pliable strength, she is thin but broad, in profile she's hardly there, but in front of me, above me, she eclipses the room — now she is above me and i am pulling myself up to her for kisses, to have my face against her hot cheek, to burn my hands on her back, to feel her lips again on my face; she is so tall that when she pins me down i am dwarfed, we are wrestling and she is on my stomach, her breast are so small and firm they don't even have a cut, they reach out hesitantly like a child taking their first steps, do not reach too far and remain close to the heart, sand dunes with snow-caps — i swear nipples go straight to the soul; tongue to touch, a soft breath against them and i am possessed by her feeling, she is kissing my neck, the muscle on the back of my shoulder, i want to scream but murmur some soft ecstatic that stretches my mouth instead, i'm half-way between sitting and lying and fall back down, she lays herself on me, kissing my shoulders, my chest, my nipples, our lips, the back of my neck, her face pressed between my head and the mattress, pressing into the nooks i feel her down my spine whether she moves from my neck or not, my mouth is spread, relaxed as if feeling alone takes every ounce of my energy, until i see her shoulder; i run my open mouth slowly across it from the nape of her neck then back to the places i'm already missing, ever so slowly, then closing down as if i may be able to swallow her, as if i can actually consume her, as if we were both not already completely consumed, flip, without thought i have spun her below me, i am back softly closing my lips around her eyebrows, down her neck, her nipples softly breathing, her stomach, opening the curtain of her legs, overtaken completely by desire i am beyond any comprehensible thought (what dreams would be in the abstract, without images), i am carried by her desire, by her breathing mixed with murmurs and bursts of something verging on laughter, her thighs, the back of her knee, nipping, kissing, licking as an animal to their wounds, how can such raging be so tender, this is real, this Is — my hair is grabbed, i am pulled to her welcoming face, glowing contentment, waiting to burst, to dive inside of me and tickle me, to feel me giggling from the inside, some suicidal dance that raises ten million souls from rest to rejoicing, to scream and make the world move, there is an indescribable pressure, a pressure she feels exactly as i do, a pressure we feel alike, starting in the middle of our bodies and breaking out like branches of a tree reaching, stretching out for sun and air, we are so stunned we cannot kiss and our lips rest on one another, we have to keep remembering to open our eyes... their is a sound that fills the room and we nearly laugh as we realize in unison that it is our own voices in some low open hum just above our breath; the pressure gives in tiny increments of ecstasy, of life (there is no question how this act can give life), each tiny bit creates more distance from every thing/feeling/thought we've ever known, we are quiet, we are one; she tells me to stop and holds me there, she holds me there as we try to grasp how we are feeling the way we are feeling, no, as we are simply overwhelmed by feeling, she whispers sshh; sshhh, and kisses my eyelids, my tears, my love, hours have passed since we entered this room, why can i do her no justice, my life to do her justice, her eyes are so open, i kiss her lids, her eyebrows, the bridge as if they were my own lips, we nip, we play, we disappear completely from this place together, she flips me over, her body is so long, she is such a landscape, the mountains, she is the horizon that mankind has worshiped as long as it has existed — it seems there is no position, no object that she could not emulate, but no, never an object, never an object, she could not be a diamond or an hourglass, she could be a waterfall, no, she could make a waterfall, she could be a river, she could be the clouds if they weren't so ethereal, the sun if it could wrap itself around you, if it could stretch and mold to its own will, she could be a leopard or a lion, most certainly a lion, sauntering one moment and the next a mile away, but she is, she can, she must be herself because while she may be any of these things they could never be her, she is here, she is real, she is firm, pure tangible, elastic, kinesthesiac; she is a heart — she is real above me dancing her movements which come from nowhere but carry a soft slow rhythm, a french horn, Coltrane, velvet and in bloom, she is removing me from my body through hers, she wants me, she wants me in a way no one ever has and i want her to take me, i want to wrap every good thing i've ever felt, ever known, ever might perceive around her, envelop her in it like some swaddled bliss as she floats down to me, touches her lips to mine, slides them gently across my neck and to my ear to whisper with hardly a hint of voice i want you to come inside of me; down my chest and she is hovering above me again, a golden idol i think i can only worship but here she is, connected to me, wanting me, my (our) breath is running (and returning), my voice is gasping (as if in tears), she is laughing herself, gripping me tight, definitely pulling me and i will go wherever she wants, and am capable — feel capable for the first time in my life of ANYTHING, and i am crying, tears running into my hair (water and breath making fire), so full of loving, so full of things i've never felt, so full there is nothing for me to do but shatter, open and let everything rush in and out, i am laughing, crying, rumbling, bothered that my body is not a forest fire, the ocean, a hurricane, i feel, i feel and am screaming now, screaming my throat tightens, eyes squinting, face convulsing hard between shut and completely open, my mouth excruciating some odd variation of lock-jaw, i can't scream, some kind of breathing-squeak-gasp is all that comes out and continues for an eternity, crazy ecstatic convulsions, crushing her in my hold while she is deep inside the woods calling me, singing to me in some moss-lullaby, some dreamy harness, squeezing me in the same way, our vitality is escaping with our breath, it hits the ceiling and mists back down on us as our sweat, makes our skin shimmer and tingle, glow fiery in the candlelight, this cannot stop, we are dumb, i am sure the world has ceased to exist, that it was all a nightmare, we are the clouds ever slowly rolling and transforming into everything that ever existed, all water has returned to fire and is rising to meet us, to merge with US, utter perfection, vibrant and immaculate, tearful and rejoicing, empowered and split open to supersede all that has existed and fucked up — we are hope, we are the most raging hope that's ever been, we could pass the world like a pebble swallowed on a dare —

Matthew Howe

Matthew Howe has been writing all his life, but now makes a living as a freelance film/video director of photography. In the recent past, he has written/produced and/or photographed 11 independent features. *Shatterdead* (videographer) and *Original Sins* (Co-writer/producer/director, videographer) are neat little genre pictures. Besides two worthy "art" pictures, the rest, he says, are foreign market action crap with God-awful names like *Airboss* and *Covert Justice*. The timid market dictates that nothing truly bizarre or interesting is ever allowed into these films. Making them is an exercise in mind-crushing tedium. To save his soul, when not busy filming on aircraft carriers, in nuclear subs or at Navy SEAL live fire exercises, he's been writing fiction.

"The Pear" was originally printed in issue 18, volume I

The Pear
by Matthew Howe

The call came in halfway through a gray Tuesday morning. Len heard it from his desk as Katie 3.0, the chipper secretary computer, answered the phone.

"Hi, thank you for calling Tortureco. How can I help you?" A slight pause as Katie's CPU decoded incoming verbal information, processed it and formulated a response. "Of course, we'd be happy to help. Now, is the purpose of the session punishment, or information extraction?"

Punishment, Len silently prayed. Then the master computer could assign any half-assed rookie. If it was an info extract, he was the only competent Rep on duty at the moment and would get the assignment. Len was tired, he'd been up half the night fighting with his wife, and just didn't feel up to it.

"Ummm hmmm." Katie murmured. "An information extraction. Very important you say. I see. I see. Well, let's just see who we have on duty today. OK?"

Len reached for his kit.

—∞—

He adjusted his hood and stared at himself in the dressing room mirror. It was not an inspiring sight. Len was wearing a cone shaped black "executioner's" hood and was bare-chested, in accordance with company policy, which was too damn bad as his chest was not much to look at these days. Pushing 40, with a few too many after work beers, he was going soft around the middle. The once firm muscle of his upper body was beginning to sag into, he was forced to admit, man tits.

He sighed, realizing how silly the whole getup was. Of course, he had to wear the hood, neither client nor subject was allowed to see his face — no one, not even his wife, knew what he actually did for a living — but the shirtless bit was taking things a little too far.

Len eyed the mirror a moment longer, reflecting on the path that had lead him here. A BA in Art History, Len had created his Senior Thesis VR on medieval torture implements as art. After college, broke and with few prospects, he had fallen into a day job as a dominator at a trendy S and M coffee bar. He had gotten into it immediately, experiencing an electric connection with the work. Word of his enthusiasm spread, luring droves of patrons to the bar and finally a visit from a Tortureco headhunter. The headhunter offered training, a high salary, benefits and a "front" career as a software consultant. What the hell, he'd signed up.

But after 14 years, it was wearing thin. Len wanted to chuck it all, take the money he had saved up and buy a place in the country. His wife was the problem; a hotshot lawyer with a downtown firm, she had little interest in leaving the city. That's what last night's fight had been about.

Len opened his case and carefully checked over his instruments. Sick of it all or not, he still considered himself a professional.

—∞—

Kendra was sweating, the room unnaturally hot. She was tied, spread-eagle and nude, to a cheesy vinyl couch. The damp skin of her back and ass were sticking to the couch making her extremely uncomfortable. She cursed the day she had ever opted to become a professional corporate spy. Sure, it had been a blast — action, secrecy, false identities — right up to her latest score, which could have been her biggest coup, but somehow went disastrously bad. She had been chased down in the street like a common criminal, abducted and dragged back here for a company-sanctioned torture session.

The door opened and the Torture Rep, a burly, frightening ogre, stepped into the room. He laid eyes on her and she detected the subtlest of hesitation on his part. She grinned inwardly even as terror began a dull drumbeat in her groin. In her late 30's, she still had a pretty rocking body, and it seemed that the Rep had taken notice. Perhaps she could use that against him somehow.

That small triumph instantly turned to nausea. Rape was considered a legitimate torture method, provided the Rep signed an affidavit claiming he took no sexual pleasure in the act. Kendra suddenly wished she were forty pounds heavier and covered with hairy moles.

The Rep moved over slowly, his eyes playing carefully over her body.

He sat next to her. She could see his eyes, hard, diamond chips leering through slits in the hood. He spoke, his voice heavily masked with digital distortion.

"You cannot win." He said simply. "There is no human alive who does not have a threshold of pain at which he or she will crack."

She ignored him, he was quoting from the Tortureco handbook.

"By law, our session will run seven hours. If I have not broken you in that time, you will be free to return to your parent corporation."

She nodded, understanding better than he knew. If she couldn't ride this out, she was finished.

But if she held out, she'd be a hero, promotions, bonuses, and assignments to the cream of the caseload. Her career would be made.

The Rep spoke again, slowly. There was a strange stammer in his voice. "I am legally obligated to disclose that in one thousand, three hundred and fifty-six sessions, I have never been beaten. Seven victims were freed prematurely due to the intercession of liberator teams. Fifty-six victims were freed prematurely due to negotiations. But no one has ever completed an entire session intact. Please. Make it easy on yourself."

"Go to hell," She said. "I'm obligated by my contract with Halycon Incorporated to make a best reasonable effort to resist all information extraction techniques used against me. I am also obligated to inform you that I have been conditioned to resist physical pain."

The Rep sighed. His entire body sagged, the folds of his ample belly seeming to collapse in on themselves. "Please," he said again. "I would rather not have to hurt you." There was real sadness in his voice, evident even through the digital masking. Kendra hardened herself to it. It was another gambit, a way of making her form some kind of bond with her tormentor. A not uncommon occurrence, she had learned.

The Rep turned to the wall-mounted clock and hit a switch. It began running, second by plodding second, toward the seven-hour session maximum. The clock was being monitored by both sides in the dispute; it could not be tampered with.

The Rep opened his case. He removed something from within and slowly raised it to eye level. Kendra sighed in relief when she saw it was only a blindfold.

"I don't want it," she said.

He tied it on, anyway. She realized why. Without being able to see him, she wouldn't know when and where the pain would be coming from. She felt panic rise within her. Kendra fought it down with the deep breathing techniques, similar to those used by women in childbirth, she had been taught during her intensive training program back at Halycon.

But while blind, she could still hear. She heard him rustling in his case.

—∞—

An alligator clip on each nipple fed short, powerful electric shocks into her tender breasts at unpredictable intervals. Kendra breathed, visualizing her focal point: a beach in New Iraq, the sun hot on her back, the gulls squeaking in the air behind her. She was nude on the sand. Crabs had crawled on her and were pinching her nipples with their tiny claws. It hurt at first, but as she breathed, and stared into a cobalt sky, the pain faded.

She grinned inwardly, the techniques were working.

Suddenly, she gasped. She heard sizzling flesh. Smelled the sick stench of it. Something red hot, a soldering iron perhaps, was on her. He was painting lines of fire across her abdomen and down her legs. She felt fear, choked it down, keeping her mind focused on the visit with the docbots she was legally entitled to at the end of the session. All physical damage would be repaired at the client's expense. She almost laughed. Maybe they could nip off a little of the cellulite that was gathering on her thighs while they were at it.

The thought broke the pain's spell and she knew she had beaten it. That thought brought new terror and she began to wince again, as she had been taught, hoping to convince the Rep that she was still suffering. The longer she could make each torture last, the better chance she had of surviving the entire session.

But he knew she was faking, almost immediately. She felt the soldering iron kiss her flesh for the last time. Kendra sighed, gathering her energy for the next round.

—∞—

He moved on to her teeth, exposing the nerve of a molar and having at it with an ultrasonic cleaning tool. Her head vibrated, a bell struck with a giant's hammer. And then it stopped. She collapsed back to the wet couch, breathing in a harsh "hee, hee, hee" pattern.

"Make me stop," he whispered.

She spat tooth powder. "Go to hell."

—∞—

Babies crying. Ear splitting screams at over 140 decibels blasted through headphones until her eardrums seemed they would burst. The cries not only tormented her ears but tore at her soul and she found herself suddenly weeping, regretting not having any children of her own.

—∞—

Acupuncture probes were screwed into ganglia, low frequency atonal harmonics surging through the probes in a precisely calculated sequence that bathed her nervous system in acid, and made her sick to her stomach. She puked, spraying everywhere, hoping through the pain that she got some on him.

—∞—

And all through it, that polite, soft voice, begging her to give in.

And through it all, the techniques she had been taught, distancing herself from the pain until a new onslaught dragged her kicking and screaming back to her battered body.

—∞—

Eons later, the blindfold came off. Kendra lay, shivering and gagging as she surveyed the wreck of her body.

He regarded her through his eye slits. She looked away, giving him nothing. He hadn't broken her. She focused on that. He hadn't broken her.

"Is it..." she croaked.

He nodded. "You have beaten me..."

She felt her heart leap and gave a gasp of triumph. She tugged at the bonds still holding her to the bed. "Come on. Get me the hell out of here."

The Rep only stared at her.

"You know the rules, you bastard. You don't break me, I get to go free." She felt a surging elation and yanked harder at her bonds.

"...so far," he whispered.

Her heart froze. "What?"

"You have beaten me...so far," he repeated and nodded to the clock behind him. The red, glaring numbers were hot pokers to her brain. 05:55:07. Still over an hour to go.

"You bastard," she whispered as her heart sank. She had fallen for the oldest ruse in the book: false hope. She felt her inner resolve dissolve. She had considered herself so strong and competent, and yet, he had fooled her with a schoolboy's trick.

Her flesh leapt as something touched her. A warm finger, she realized. She looked down as the Rep began to gently trace the lines of her body, skipping over the burned, bloody portions.

"You've done well," he said, "Six hours is quite an achievement. I've used nearly every technique modern science has devised, and yet, you resist. Your training is excellent."

She spat blood at him. It landed in a gob on his hood and dripped — a crimson tear.

"But the techniques you've been taught are relatively new, the science of pain control is in its infancy. The science of pain infliction, on the other hand, is so very old."

He reached into his case and came up with something that clanked gently in his grasp. He held it out before her — a proud daddy cradling his newborn. It was a rusty, oblong piece of metal with an ornate, flat handle sticking out of its back end. "This is one of the old ways. There is little science here, just brute vulgarity. It is called the pear."

She nodded, seeing at once that it did resemble a pear.

"Is it..." she cursed herself for speaking.

He nodded. "The real thing. Over 600 years old."

She stared at the rusty, flaking surface. It was the foulest thing she had ever seen.

"It's quite simple." He said quietly. "Insert the pear into the body orifice of choice, and turn the handle." He turned the handle. The pear gave an evil, shrieking squeal and split into quarters, each hinged at the base, opening like a four-petaled flower.

"It will expand to several times its original size inside you. And when your pain has reached its peak, I pull it out. Slowly."

Kendra began to shiver.

"I hate to use it, the chance of damaging the mechanism, you know...and it is an antique..."

She said nothing, staring at the implement.

"But, you leave me no choice."

He touched the pear to her chest, directly between her breasts, and slowly dragged it down her abdomen. Even through her pain, she could feel it scrape along her skin, which instantly broke out in goosebumps. It left a rusty trail in her sweat, a dull red line more horrific than blood.

It rode up and over the folds of her abdomen, then disappeared between her legs. She felt it trail down her left inner thigh, pause at the inside of the knee, then cruise slowly back up.

It paused at the apex. Kendra found herself shivering violently, eyes jammed shut.

She felt the rusty metal's kiss.

Kendra screamed.

Kendra babbled names, places, drop locations, everything, over and over, as she wept and begged and pleaded for him to take it away.

The Rep turned and packed his gear as the lawyers charged in to take her statement.

—∞—

A woman's scream woke Len from a sound slumber. "Lights on, 20 percent," he murmured. The room brightened to a dull glow as he turned to face his wife, who was thrashing in their bed, caught in the grip of a feverish nightmare.

Len reached for her, and woke her. Kendra calmed slowly in his strong arms.

"Are you all right?" he asked.

"Yes, I'm...just a nightmare."

Len nodded. She'd have them every few days for the next month or so, then they'd slowly fade.

He saw Kendra staring at her hands and her thighs. He had made sure the docbots had done their work properly at session's end. There were no scars. Nothing to contradict her story that the day had been just another long day at the office.

"Is there something bothering you?" he asked.

"No, no, just...work. I'm under a lot of pressure right now."

"Big case?" he asked.

She nodded hurriedly. He pulled her close.

"You know," she said softly. "Sometimes I think we should just drop it all, these stupid jobs we both have, move out to the country. Live off our investments. Start a family. Do you ever think like that?"

He held her closer. "Sometimes."

THE END

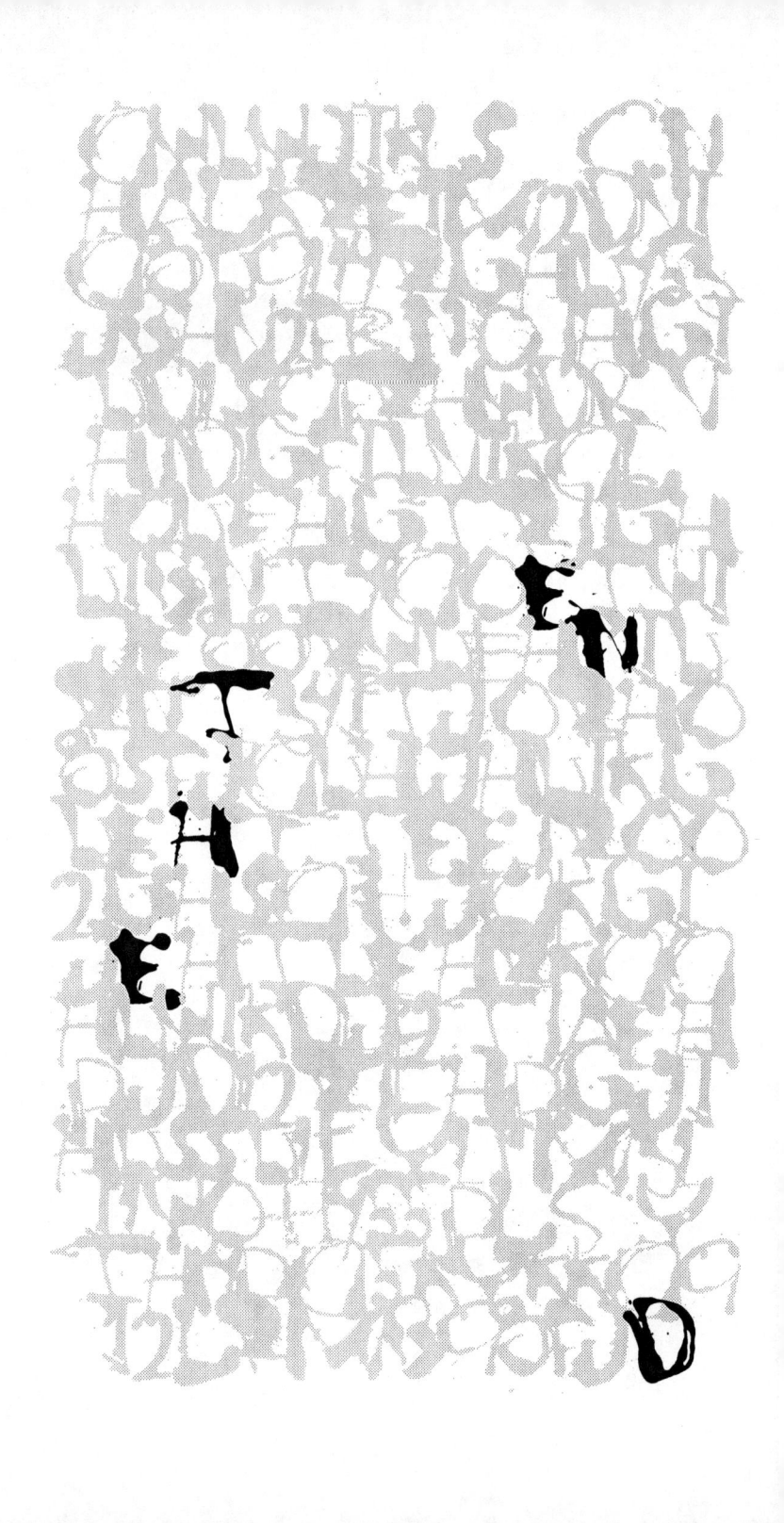

GET SOME TODAY!
CthulhuSex
Blood, Sex and Tentacles
The Magazine for Connoisseurs of Sensual Horror

"Cthulhu Sex Magazine is a haven for Lovecraft fans both new & old. Wrap your tentacles around this ASAP!"

STEVE "UNCLE CREEPY" BARTON
— *The Horror Channel*

BENEATH THE COVER OF EACH ISSUE, EXPLORE THRILLING WORKS FROM SUCH MASTERS AS

H. R. GIGER,
C. J. HENDERSON,
MARK MCLAUGHLIN,
PAUL KOMODA,
CHRISTINE MORGAN,
ALLEN KOSZOWSKI,
WRATH JAMES WHITE

AND MANY MORE.

PICK UP *Cthulhu Sex Magazine* AT A NEWSSTAND NEAR YOU OR GET IT ONLINE AT:
WWW.CTHULHUSEX.COM

ONLY $4.95* PER ISSUE
OR $15.00* SUBSCRIPTION

FOR MORE INFORMATION ON *Cthulhu Sex Magazine*, VISIT WWW.CTHULHUSEX.COM OR SEND A SASE TO
Cthulhu Sex Magazine
PO BOX 3678, GRAND CENTRAL STATION
NEW YORK, NY 10163

Cthulhu Sex
MAGAZINE
WWW.CTHULHUSEX.COM

RICES GIVEN ARE FOR CONTINENTAL US ORDERS ONLY AND SUBJECT TO CHANGE WITHOUT NOTICE.

RAW DOG SCREAMING PRESS

100 Jolts 156 pages, $12.95
One hundred short shots of fiction guaranteed to
From his hilarious satire on technical manuals, "Sta
for Dummies," to a sharp series of "Skull Fragm
vignettes Arnzen proves he has honed his cr
deliver the highest voltage using the fewest word

A Dirge for the Temporal 208 pages, $14.95
Prepare for a decadant feast. Darren Speegle's se
collection of fiction, bursts with sensations.
Baroque architecture, plush velvet furnishings o
richest chocolate truffle dessert, Speegle's prose de
all the senses.

This collection heralds the return of the subtly cr
horror tale. *A Dirge* lingers on the dark mystery c
supernatural, creates the giddy feeling of fear mixed
excitement, that only comes from partial revela
things half-glimpsed and misty.

Old world legend and gothic sensibilities lurk be
every corner. A world of aching beauty and imper
doom awaits. Speegle's work is a rare treat to be sav

Sick 296 pages, $15.95
The world of publishing has just received its bill of h
and the prognosis isn't pretty. Literary marauders are
up from the hazardous material bins labeled Ho
Surrealism, & Science Fiction. Here the pen is not n
mightier than the sword; it is a plague heralding the a
lypse for convention, writing a dirge for complac
These Sick stories are horrendous and hilarious disse
of creative minds on the scalpel's edge.

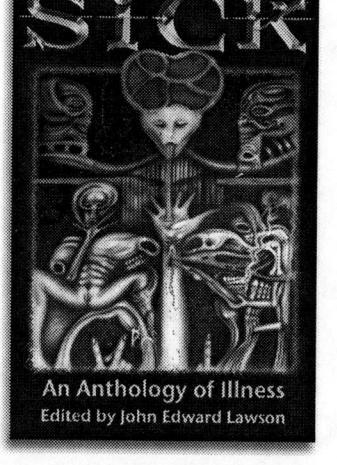

I suggest you slap a stamp on the cover that reads: SURG
GENERAL'S WARNING: Reading this book may cause
tal deficits, breakdowns, manias, and could induce the r
to grope strangers and utter sexual innuendoes at ina
priate public venues." —Michael Hemmingson

www.rawdogscreaming.com

Everybody Scream! 292 pages, $15.95

Thomas first seduced readers to the world of Punktown through a short story collection of the same name, bending time and technology to create a futuristic world real as our own. *Everybody Scream!* continues the seduction with characters every bit as vibrant only this time each person's story collides with the others in a dizzying thrill-ride of a novel.

The final day of the season for the annual Punktown Fair excitement runs high. For those in charge, Del and Sophi Kahn, it's a bittersweet day of transition. Little do they realize how severely this one day will test their relationship. In fact, it's a catalyst for many Punktown residents; drawing them in, stirring them up and letting them loose on each other.

This roller coaster tale builds to a peak of expectation then plummets, twisting and turning, a breathtaking juggernaut to the final chapters with plenty of screams and giggles along the way.

"...an intricate and thoroughly engrossing world, one that digs deep and lingers."

— Carlton Mellick III

Also from Two Backed Books

Tempting Disaster 260 pages, $16.95

Tempting Disaster is an anthology from the edge that examines our culture's obsession with sexual taboos. Postmodernists and surrealists have banded together with renegade horror and sci-fi authors to re-envision what is "erotic" and what is "acceptable." By turns humorous and horrific, shocking and alluring, the authors dissect those impulses we deny in our daily lives.

Preying on all known fetishes — and even inventing some new kinks along the way this literary experimentation on human desire results in what can only be described as the ultimate *Tempting Disaster*. Includes stories by Michael Hemmingson, Lance Olsen, Jeffrey Thomas & Carlton Mellick III.

www.twobackedbooks.com

Printed in the United States
62209LVS00002B/91